Weird U.S.
A FREAKY FIELD TRIP
THROUGH THE 50 STATES

by Matt Lake and Randy Fairbanks

STERLING CHILDREN'S BOOKS
New York

STERLING CHILDREN'S BOOKS
New York

An Imprint of Sterling Publishing
387 Park Avenue South
New York, NY 10016

To my parents, for raising a handful of weird kids who turned out all right —Matt

To my mother, who bought me my first subscription to *Famous Monsters of Filmland* —Randy

Library of Congress Cataloging-in-Publication Data

Lake, Matthew.
   Weird U.S. : a freaky field trip through the 50 states / Matt Lake and
Randy Fairbanks.
      p. cm.
   Includes index.
   ISBN 978-1-4027-5462-3
   1. Curiosities and wonders — United States — Juvenile literature. 2.
United States — Miscellanea — Juvenile literature. 3. United
States — Guidebooks — Juvenile literature. 4. United
States — History — Miscellanea — Juvenile literature. 5. Folklore—United
States — Juvenile literature. I. Fairbanks, Randy. II. Title.
   E179.L22 2011
   973--dc22
                                      2010027019
Lot#: 10 9 8 7 6 5 4 3 2 1
03/11

Published by Sterling Publishing Co., Inc.
387 Park Avenue South, New York, NY 10016
© 2011 by Mark Sceurman and Mark Moran

Distributed in Canada by Sterling Publishing
C/o Canadian Manda Group, 165 Dufferin Street Toronto, Ontario, Canada M6K 3H6

Distributed in the United Kingdom by GMC Distribution Services
Castle Place, 166 High Street, Lewes, East Sussex, England BN7 1XU

Distributed in Australia by Capricorn Link (Australia) Pty. Ltd.
P.O. Box 704, Windsor, NSW 2756, Australia

Printed in China

Sterling ISBN 978-1-4027-5462-3

Photography and illustration credits are found on page 127 and constitute an extension of this copyright page.

For information about custom editions, special sales, premium andcorporate purchases, please contact
Sterling Special SalesDepartment at 800-805-5489 or specialsales@sterlingpublishing.com.

Designed by Anke Stohlmann Design.

This book is intended as entertainment to present a historical record of local legends, folklore, and sites throughout the United States of America. Many of these legends and stories cannot be independently confirmed or corroborated, and the authors and publisher make no representation as to their factual accuracy. The reader should be advised that some of the sites described in this book are located on private property and should not be visited without permission, or you may face prosecution for trespassing.

CONTENTS

GET READY FOR ONE VERY WEIRD ROAD TRIP

Imagine yourself traveling through all fifty states in the U.S. You'd see oceans, mountains, majestic plains, Mount Rushmore, the Empire State Building, Old Faithful, and so much more. You'd hear about our nation's founders, its war heroes, and others who made our country the awesome place it is today. Along the way, you might pull over at a rest stop or convenience store and overhear someone talking about the biggest catsup bottle in the U.S. Your parents don't want to fall behind schedule, but they notice how excited you are about seeing it. "What the heck, let's do it!" says Dad. Next thing you know, you're staring up at a 170-foot water tower shaped like a catsup bottle. There's no souvenir shop there—just the giant catsup bottle.

Now imagine a whole cross-country trip that skips the major tourist attractions and stops only at the weird, freaky, and unbelievable places, where you hear all about the weird, freaky creatures that haunt towns across the country. Perhaps you also catch a couple of ghost stories and even meet a wacky guy who may seem strange to some but is just as important to the United States as all those normal people we read about in history books (who, by the way, weren't all that normal!). That's what this book is all about. Forget the tourist attractions with the long lines and whiny babies, and bring on the weird, the wild, the unconfirmed, the unbelievable!

Weird Central

Before we take you from sea to shining sea bringing you the weirdest America has to offer, we should introduce ourselves. We're two beat writers at Weird Central, which is a mysterious base (located somewhere in the swamps of Jersey) where news of all the weird things in the U.S. eventually ends up. Imagine a small, cramped office with phones ringing off the hooks; e-mails coming in by the thousands from correspondents from all fifty states checking in with new weird stories; and vast data banks of weirdness whirring and clicking with up-to-the-minute news of UFOs, giant fiberglass statues by the side of the road, strange burial sites, ghosts, aliens, and people who parade the streets for very strange reasons. Well, Weird Central is nothing like that, but we do collect these stories, and we've put the best of them in this book.

You'll meet monsters! You'll visit creepy museums! Watch out for ghosts!

Located in **Collinsville, Illinois**, the Brooks catsup bottle goes great with the giant hot dogs on page 51.

Welcome to Weird U.S.!

Did we miss your favorite story? Write to us and let us know. The weird will never run out completely, and we have plans to deliver it to you in a whole series of Weird U.S. books. Just watch and wait—and send us your stories! We know they're out there.

MYSTERIOUS MUSEUMS & CURIOUS COLLECTIONS

maybe it's because we enjoyed field trips so much when we were in school, but one of our favorite activities is jumping in the Weirdmobile and going to a museum. As you can imagine though, the museums we visit aren't like the ones your teachers take you to (unless they have a Weirdbus). From displays housed in buildings to curious collections in people's homes, we've visited museums all over Weird America, and we're proud to present our own little "museum" of museums that make us scratch our heads and say, "What in the world is going on here?"

Curiouser and Curiouser

If you're shopping for a friend's birthday gift at Ye Olde Curiosity Shop in **Seattle, Washington**, you may feel like someone—or something—is staring at you. That someone is probably Sylvester or one of the many other mummies or shrunken heads on display here. You see, Ye Olde Curiosity Shop is a store that's dressed up as a museum. (Or is it the other way around?) It's been around for a hundred years, and from the start it has displayed some really odd items that are not for sale, right next to things with price tags on them. The first owner, Joseph Standley, collected bizarre items—baskets made of armadillo hide, a walrus skull with three tusks, and a two-headed calf—which he put next to the items he was actually selling. And it worked! His bizarre idea caught on, and people came to gawk and buy. Now, Ye Olde Curiosity Shop is a tourist destination for anyone who wants to look at the mummies and shrunken heads as they shop.

In fact, there's too much weird for one store. Right next to Ye Olde Curiosity Shop on Pier 54 on Seattle's waterfront is its spin-off—Ye Olde Curiosity Shop Too. That's two weird places for the price of one . . . and that's what we call a bargain.

Sorry, Not for Sale

What are you looking at?

Check it out!
www.yeoldecuriosityshop.com

7

Rodent Resurrection

Lots of museums have stuffed animals in them, and nobody thinks twice about how strange it is. Most grown-ups say, "Oh, that's just taxidermy," and pass it off as normal. So it takes a special kind of museum to make taxidermy seem truly weird. That's why we like the Dead Pals of Sam Sanfillippo in **Madison, Wisconsin**. For one thing, all of its inhabitants are smaller than us—there are no creepy glass-eyed bears or tigers here to loom over us with their teeth showing. And even better, these little stuffed rodents are all mounted in strange and silly ways. Gray squirrels sit around a poker table playing cards. Chipmunks sit on stools made of bottles. One suave-looking squirrel sits in front of a tiny grand piano in front of a mirror. And a cool albino squirrel sits in a brightly colored Barbie car.

This curious collection is the work of a retired funeral home director named Sam Sanfillippo, which is why the whole thing is on display in a funeral home. You can see Mr. Sanfillippo's work at the Cress Funeral Home. It's free to get in, but you should check in advance because the museum is closed if there's a funeral.

Abita Mystery House

If you ever get to **Abita Springs, Louisiana**, look for the UCM Museum. The letters don't stand for anything—but the museum certainly does. It stands for very, very weird art, and it's known as Louisiana's most eccentric museum. Even the buildings are odd. This museum is made up of an old-timey gas station and a collection of metal-sided sheds covered with flagpoles that have bicycle wheels on them instead of flags.

The first American museums were little more than large boxes that were taken from town to town. Once opened (for a small fee) these boxes were like junk drawers of wonder, containing an odd mixture of real and fake artifacts from arrowheads and fossils to ancient Roman coins, shrunken heads, and just about anything else. As museums became more established and began focusing more on education, they lost some of that sense of wonder of the traveling museums.

Check it out!
www.ucmmuseum.com

It's even stranger inside. There are wild (and fake) hybrid creatures such as Buford the bassigator (half giant fish, half alligator), Darrell the dogigator (half dog, half alligator), and a unique mermaid with an alligator's body instead of a fish tail. There's also a collection of pottery, a hand-cranked organ, and a miniature village. But just as you start to think you're getting used to the level of weird in this museum, along comes something even more unusual—like the old barn covered with more than 15,000 pieces of broken crockery, called the House of Shards, or the old-fashioned, metallic mobile home with a UFO stuck in its side. All this for the price of a family sized bag of chips!

The Allen County Museum in **Lima, Ohio**, is filled to the gills with all sorts of historical oddities, including an exhibit of swallowed objects that were removed from people's esophagi, lungs, and larynges. The collection includes a diaper pin, buttons, dentures, coins, bones, a key, and a piece of rubber hose. Check it out at www.allencountymuseum.org!

Museum of Jurassic Technology

Not all museums are real. Some contain real-looking things, but they are full of jokes that many grown-ups just don't get. But we get them, and so will you. The Museum of Jurassic Technology in **Culver City, California**, is one of these joke museums. Even the name is a contradiction. There was no technology in the Jurassic era. Even those smart velociraptors in the movies couldn't actually build anything. And everything else at the time was basically raptor bait.

You'll see genuine works of art here, including sculptures on the tops of needles that are so tiny you need a magnifying glass to see them. Then there are fakes such as the diorama on the Cameroonian stink ant. There's also a sculpture gallery dedicated to unusual cures for common illnesses. For example: a mouse pie that cures the whooping cough (it doesn't). Or a duck that looks like it's kissing someone, because duck's breath cures sore throats (no way). But no matter. It's all part of the fun!

Check it out! www.mjt.org

International Cryptozoology Museum

Once located in Loren Coleman's house, this museum is now in downtown **Portland, Maine**, just down the street from the world-famous Portland Museum of Art. One of the first things you'll notice is an eight-foot, four-hundred-pound Bigfoot statue. And that's just the beginning of the monsters. The place also has models of the Mothman (see page 74), the Loch Ness Monster, and one or two suspect specimens that you'll meet in the Creepy Creature Expedition chapter (see page 68), including jackalopes, the FeeJee mermaid, and the infamous furry trout. There are also movie and TV costumes, including some from the classic of the silver screen *The Mothman Prophecies*, and a twenty-two-foot thunderbird from the TV series *FreakyLinks*.

But this place isn't just a zoological joke. You'll also see a real six-foot fish called a coelacanth, which was presumed extinct for sixty-five million years until someone found a live one swimming around in 1938. There are also lots of skulls from prehistoric people—Gigantopithecus, Australopithecus, and Heidelberg Man—and various apes and monkeys. If you're more of a cat fan, the museum has skulls from all kinds of lions and other fearsome felines.

Check it out!

www.cryptozoologymuseum.com

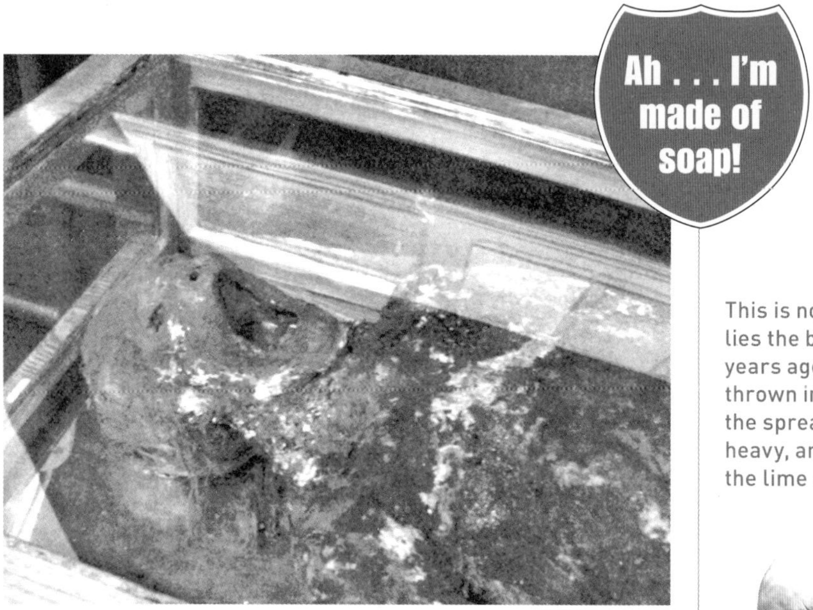
Ah . . . I'm made of soap!

This is not your normal, everyday mummy. Inside the display lies the body of a woman who lived more than a hundred years ago. In those days, a caustic powder called lime was thrown into graves before they were filled in. This prevented the spread of disease. However, this woman was pretty heavy, and a strange chemical reaction took place between the lime and her body fat. It turned her into soap!

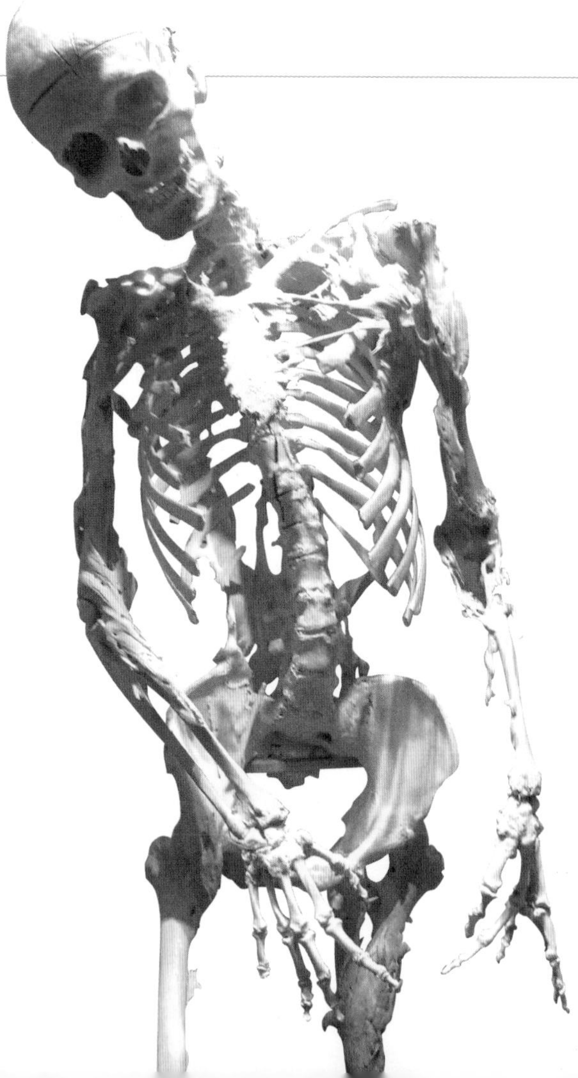

The Mütter Museum

Teachers love science museums. But not every science museum contains exhibits that you'd ever be tested on. Medical museums exhibit things that can freak you out if you look at them too closely. For example, you don't want to go to the Mütter (pronounced "mooter") Museum. Let your Weirdmobile drive right on past. We've been there and spent a lot of time catching sight of things that made us turn the other way. This gross-out gallery is a collection of medical teaching exhibits attached to Philadelphia's College of Physicians. The exhibits are designed not only to teach trainee doctors about illnesses but also to gross them out so much that they'll never look shocked in front of their patients. So trust us when we tell you not to visit. However, if you want to impress your friends and older relatives, tell them about some of the less gruesome exhibits on the next page so they'll think you've been there. We won't let on.

Check it out! www.collphyphil.org

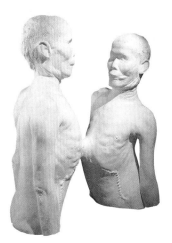

Scientists call twins who are connected to each other "conjoined twins." Ever wonder why everyone else calls them "Siamese twins"? It's because the most famous connected twins came from a country called Siam. Their names were Chang and Eng, and a plaster cast of them stands right in the middle of the museum.

How's the weather up there?

There are plenty of bones at the Mütter Museum, but the best examples are in a single case: they are the full skeletons of a giant man and a dwarf.

Back in the old days, people thought you could tell everything about a person's personality from the shape of their head. It was an idea called *phrenology*, and a smart doctor once set out to prove it was bogus. He collected skulls from all kinds of people from all over the world. These skulls now sit in a case along one wall of the Mütter Museum, each with a brief history of the person the bones once belonged to.

National Museum of Health and Medicine

The next time you go to **Washington D.C.**, see if you can get to the Walter Reed Army Medical Center. In Building 54, there's a place where big kids have been wigging out their younger siblings for years. It's the National Museum of Health and Medicine, and it's the only place we know of that features a giant hairball that was surgically removed from a twelve-year-old girl. If that isn't enough to make you beg your parents for a freaky field trip to this museum, consider another great historical exhibit: the leg of a Civil War general. On the second day of fighting at Gettysburg, Major General Daniel Sickles lost the lower half of his right leg after a cannonball hit it. But he was our kind of war hero: he mailed the leg to the Army Medical Museum with a card that read, "With the compliments of Major General D.E.S." He visited the leg at the museum every year for the rest of his life, and the shattered bones are now on display next to a cannonball.

Some of the main attractions at the Historical Dental Museum in **Philadelphia, Pennsylvania**, include old (and scary-looking) drills as well as this big bucket of teeth.

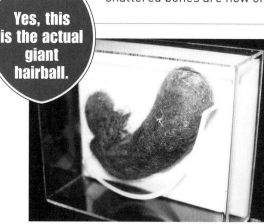

Yes, this is the actual giant hairball.

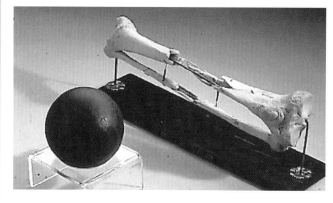

That had to have hurt.

Check it out!
www.nmhm.washingtondc.museum

Toilet Lid Decorator

It's a fact of life: when toilets go wrong, somebody has to fix them. In the **San Antonio, Texas**, area, that man used to be Barney Smith, a master plumber. If things leaked or got plugged up, Barney Smith was the man to call. But sometime around 1970, he took his professional interest in porcelain pots to a whole new level.

One day, Barney and his father returned home from a hunting trip with an impressive set of antlers each. His father mounted his set to a traditional plaque. For a laugh, Barney fixed his antlers onto a toilet seat lid. He liked the results so much he decided to make a few more examples of potty seat art. In fact, for the next twenty years, he stuck anything that struck his fancy to wooden toilet seats and their lids. When he was done, he placed the results on the walls of his garage.

In the early 1990s, he took his collection public, and from that point onward, Barney Smith's garage has become an attraction to weird-loving visitors who can feast their eyes on eyeglasses, electronics, sports memorabilia, wooden nickels, and 700 other examples of decorated toilet seat covers. Barney insists that the one he actually uses for its original purpose is an ordinary plastic one.

If you visit the National Museum of Dentistry in **Baltimore, Maryland** you'll get to see George Washington's false teeth. Legend says he had wooden teeth, but this museum knows better. In fact, Washington's dentures are much weirder. For one thing, the "teeth" are actually carved bits of elk bone. They're set in a gold plate that was beaten into the shape of Washington's gums. The top and bottom plates of these false teeth were connected by a coiled spring. The next time you look at George Washington on a dollar bill, look closely at his frowning mouth with his lower lip sticking out. He had to keep his lower lip tight so the springs wouldn't shoot the lower set of dentures straight out of his mouth!
Check it out at www.dentalmuseum.org.

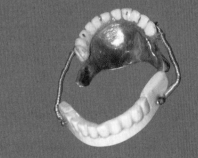

Much like our nation's first president, these dentures were ready to spring into action.

Celebrity Bites

Steve Jenne's collection is a bit unusual even by Weird standards. In fact, it's a tad disturbing. He collects half-eaten sandwiches. To be more accurate, he collects sandwiches that have been bitten into by celebrities. Steve started his collection in 1960, when he was fourteen years old and lived in **Sullivan, Illinois**. The nation's vice president, Richard Nixon, was visiting the town, and Steve, who was part of the local Boy Scout troop, was asked to tidy up after the event. He noticed that the VP had taken only a few bites of his buffalo barbecue sandwich, so he took it home and stored it in a jar. The local newspaper wrote an article about Steve's souvenir sandwich, but for thirty years, Steve didn't think about adding to his collection. That changed in 1988 when another reporter tracked him down for a follow-up article. This second newspaper article attracted a lot of attention—and a lot more half-eaten sandwiches. The late-night chat-show host Johnny Carson gave him one. So did comedians Henny Youngman and Tiny Tim and a host of sports stars and other celebrities. Steve stores all the sandwiches—and their traces of celebrity spit—in his freezer in **Springfield, Illinois**.

Hungry yet?

The world's largest (and only) thermometer museum is in **Onset, Massachusetts**. It's in Dick Porter's basement.

The World's Greatest Wrap Artist

Here's a collection that almost nobody in the world would consider: gum wrappers. The man with the largest collection of them lives in **Virginia Beach, Virginia**, and his name is Gary Duschl. He has 1,516,102 of them—all folded into one long gum-wrapper chain. He started folding them on March 11, 1965, and he never stopped. Every year on the anniversary of the day he started, he has his chain counted and measured. At last count, it was 64,176 feet long—that's more than twelve miles, or forty-three times the size of the Empire State Building. If you laid out his gum-wrapper chain in a straight line and jumped into a car, it would take twelve minutes at sixty miles an hour to get from one end to the other. If you walked, it would take you more than five hours.

Gary's a regular guy who holds a full-time job and leads a normal life, but he just has an odd hobby that has made him into a local hero and an international celebrity. After folding gum wrappers into a chain for more than forty-five years, he got his name in the record books for having the world's longest gum wrapper chain. And he's still folding. He estimates that the chain weighs more than four full-grown men and that it's taken $105,000 worth of gum to supply the wrappers. He's quick to point out that he didn't chew it all himself. He gets donations of Wrigley wrappers from friends, neighbors, and fans of his website at www.gumwrapper.com.

Chew on this: It's taken more than $100,000 worth of gum to make this gum-wrapper chain!

STRANGE STREET GATHERINGS

just about every town in the U.S. holds annual celebrations and parades of some sort to commemorate special times. There's Independence Day, Memorial Day, New Year's, Thanksgiving, and more. But there are also towns that bring on the noise for celebrations that are a bit . . . dare we say it . . . weird. This part of the field trip takes you to ordinary places where strange celebrations and parades take place.

Need a lift?

Kinetic Sculpture Race

It's hard to beat a good bike ride in May. Summer's just a few weeks away, and people are starting to relax and have fun—especially in towns that have kinetic sculpture races. These are the silliest road races in the nation (if not the world)! Basically, people dress up their bikes to look like dragons, fish tanks, or poodles, and then race them through streets, fields, and even water. Sometimes the bikes aren't even bikes—they're custom-built, pedal-powered machines made especially for the race. And it all takes place in towns across America sometime around Memorial Day.

In the four decades since the first kinetic sculpture race, some strange rules have emerged. Racers are supposed to carry a sock puppet with them at all times. There's a honk-and-pass rule that states you must let another racer go past if he honks at you. And one of the most coveted awards is the Mediocre Award. It's awarded to the person who finishes the race exactly in the middle of the pack. If you can't manage that, being second-to-last is the next best thing.

The first kinetic sculpture race took place in **Ferndale, California**, in 1969, when Hobart Brown bolted some strange additions to his son's tricycle. Neighbors said, "I bet I could beat that weird trike in a race," and Brown rose to the challenge. Every year since, there has been a race between artistically altered cycles and their crazy drivers (who call themselves *kinetinauts*). The Ferndale race runs about forty miles to neighboring Arcata and back. Check it out at www.kineticgrandchampionship.com.

A much muddier race takes place on the shores of the reservoir in **Boulder, Colorado**. It's three miles long, but two of those miles are on water.

For about thirty years, **Baltimore, Maryland**, has held a fifteen-mile race that runs from Fort McHenry all across town to the Inner Harbor, where weird vehicles must run through a muddy stretch of the Chesapeake Bay. The American Visionary Art Museum sponsors this race, and every year, the museum enters its own vehicle—a pink poodle on wheels named Fifi.

Start Your Engines!

Anyone who's watched NASCAR knows what happens when car enthusiasts gather in one place—there's a lot of wheel squealing, engine revving, and racing in circles. That's not exactly what happens every May in **Houston, Texas**, during its annual Orange Show. That's when the art cars come out, and up to 200,000 people line the sidewalks of Allen Parkway to scratch their heads and ask, "What on earth is that?"

Art cars are exactly what they sound like: cars that have been changed around so much they don't look anything like the car your parents drive. Art cars look like they came out of someone's wildest dreams. Sometimes, the art is an incredible paint job. Sometimes, it's a collection of tinfoil and plastic fruit glued to the machine. Other times, it's a collection of Barbie dolls or a tuba fixed firmly to the roof. If you can't make it to the Art Car Weekend in May, we suggest a trip to the Art Car Museum on Heights Boulevard in Houston. It shows past entries in the Art Car Weekend and plenty of strange and wonderful art. It's nicknamed the Garage Mahal, because, well, it's a garage, and the exterior is adorned with metallic domes and spires like India's Taj Mahal.

Check it out!
www.orangeshow.org

Even my spark plugs are glittery!

Our favorite house features a large pile of hubcaps in the shape of a Christmas tree. On a cold December night, what could be better than warming your hands on the collective glow of thousands of twinkling lights?

Check it out!
www.christmasstreet.com

Miracle on 34th Street

Once Thanksgiving is over, a strange phenomenon occurs across the nation. People drape trees and windows with miles of wires with tiny lights on them. They inflate models of a large, bearded man dressed in red and place them on their front lawns. And at night, passing airplanes can see the glow of all these lights. But no street in the nation can compare to Thirty-fourth Street in **Hampden, Maryland**, during the run-up to Christmas. This street is draped with so many lights, it feels ten degrees warmer than Thirty-third and Thirty-second streets, and although we haven't checked this out ourselves, we're sure the glow it gives off can be seen from outer space.

It's called the Christmas Street or the Miracle on 34th Street, and it takes the holiday season to its logical conclusion—which means that it goes way over the top. Any one house on this street could have dozens of glowing candy canes on its steps and fifty angels on its roof. But the excesses don't stop at one house—they cover both sides of the whole block. Giant red and white lollipops stick out over picket fences. Twinkling snowflakes deck the roofs so thickly, you wonder where Santa will be able to park his sled. And although neighbors do try to outdo each other, they also cooperate: they stretch ropes of lights across the whole street so you have overhead lights whenever you visit. And people do visit—a local parade in early December attracts tens of thousands of people at once, and during the entire month of December, thousands more visit.

Even hideous holiday decorations have their place, and that place is the Aluminum Tree and Aesthetically Challenged Seasonal Ornament Museum & Research Center. It began in **Brevard, North Carolina**, as a joke. Stephen Jackson fished a single horrible-looking fake tree from a trash heap and displayed it. His collection has grown to more than sixty trees, decorated with ornaments made from curtain rings, duct tape, and other junk. The museum is open between Thanksgiving and Christmas.

Check it out!
www.aluminumtree.com

The Pirate of Hampton, Virginia

Next time you watch Johnny Depp as Captain Jack Sparrow in the *Pirates of the Caribbean* movies, remember one thing: he got his sense of style from a real-life pirate named Edward Teach, who sailed the high seas in the early 1700s. If you've never heard of Captain Teach, it's probably because he went by a much more famous nickname: Blackbeard.

Blackbeard was a larger-than-life personality. He named his ship *Queen Anne's Revenge*. He grew a beard at a time when nobody wore beards, and to make himself look even more outlandish, he braided his beard and tied it up with black ribbons. And to take things even further over the top, he sometimes set fire to the ribbons so his whole beard smoked. Yes, Blackbeard was a mighty strange man. And that's why we still celebrate him every June at the Blackbeard Pirate Festival in **Hampton, Virginia**.

Sailing ships stage historical reenactments along the shore, and crazy character actors in costume wander around. The loudest and strangest of them all is Mr. Ben Cherry,

Aargh!

"To get goods to the colonists," Ben told us, "they had to be brought in either by the English government or the pirates. Guess who brought in the most goods? The pirates!"

America's leading Blackbeard impersonator. The festival is well worth a visit, if only to hear Ben shout the praises of pirates to whoever will listen. He describes pirates as the truckers of their day. He's also known to proclaim that pirates were not nearly as bad as their reputations. "Blackbeard never took a human life," Ben said. "Blackbeard always considered himself a nonconformist. He liked to be different. He was sort of ahead of his time . . . a colorful character."

Check it out! www.blackbeardpiratefestival.com

The Legend of Blackbeard's Skull

Even though pirates like Blackbeard had their fans and supporters, pirates broke the law, and the punishment for many crimes at the time was death. After only two years of plying his trade, Blackbeard was killed in a fight with the authorities. According to legend, Lieutenant Robert Maynard cut off his head and hung it from the yard arm to warn other pirates to mend their ways. This gave rise to another legend: the fate of Blackbeard's skull. Some say his enemies covered the skull with silver and made it into a cup. Others say that his pirate buddies stole the skull from his enemies . . . and made it into a silver drinking cup. And then there's the other legend—that the skull was passed among private collectors for centuries. That's what a writer named Edward Rowe Snow claimed in 1949, when he came forward with a skull he said was Blackbeard's. He held onto the skull till he died in the late 1980s, when his widow donated it to the Peabody Essex Museum in **East India Square, Salem, Massachusetts**. That's where it remains to this day, on display for the general public.

Blobfest

What's your favorite movie of all time? Is it something set in a galaxy far, far away? In the Caribbean? In a school for wizards? Whatever it is, we're betting one thing: it's not about an oozy blob of slime in eastern Pennsylvania. But even if the 1958 science fiction/horror movie *The Blob* isn't your favorite movie, the annual festival in **Phoenixville, Pennsylvania**, near Philadelphia, might well turn into your favorite summer celebration. The movie was shot in Phoenixville, and it features events at the local diner, the local movie theater, and more than twenty other locations. The movie had a lot of screaming, so there's a screaming contest. It was a wacky science fiction story, so there's a tinfoil hat contest. There's a scene in the movie in which all the teenagers in the town run out of the Colonial Theatre to fight the Blob, so the high point of the festival is a recreation of that scene, which they call the Running-Out.

Check it out! www.thecolonialtheatre.com

Frozen Dead Guy Days

As the cold weather thaws out and spring arrives, the little town of **Nederland, Colorado** holds one of the strangest celebrations you can imagine. It's called the Frozen Dead Guy Days, and it's held in honor of a man who's frozen in a shed outside of town. When Bredo Morstoel died in 1989, his grandson didn't want to bury or cremate him, so he preserved his body in dry ice. Nederland didn't like deep-frozen guys in town, but what could they do? They couldn't pass a law to prohibit it, so in 2002, they took another approach: they held a three-day festival in his honor. And they made it an annual event. It takes place in early March and features a Slow Motion Parade (featuring antique hearses) and the Tuff Shed Coffin Race, which pits teams of colorful coffin-bearers on an icy obstacle course.

The Hobo Convention

Back in the Great Depression of the 1920s and 1930s, a group of homeless migrants crisscrossed the United States. They hitched rides on freight trains, gathered around campfires in shantytowns, and shared tips for living outside of regular society. **Britt, Iowa**, was a hub for hobos at the time, and it now boasts a hobo museum, a hobo cemetery, and an annual hobo convention. At the convention, they nominate the Hobo King and Hobo Queen for the upcoming year and pay respect to legendary hobos of days gone by. This August, if you're clamoring for something to do, why not hop a freight and make your way out to Britt? Other rail riders will be waiting!

Check it out! www.hobo.com

Check it out!
www.spamarama.org

April Fools'!

Most of us trick our friends on April 1. Two cities take the April Fool spirit one step further: **Austin, Texas**, holds a festival in honor of lunch meat, and **San Francisco, California**, sings the praises of a saint who doesn't exist. Austin's Spamarama began in 1978 when two friends, Dick Terry and David Arnsberger, decided that Texas chili cook-offs weren't the only food festivals worth having. They set up a joke festival in honor of Spam, the pink, canned, meat-like substance. On the same day about 1,700 miles west, San Francisco hosts a parade dedicated to the patron saint of the day. The Saint Stupid's Day Parade marches up to the pyramid-shaped Transamerica building, where the crowd throws pennies at a sculpture. Their explanation for this behavior? "It's a stupid coin and a stupid sculpture. What better tribute to Saint Stupid?"

The Miracle Mike Festival

Have you ever felt like you've lost your mind? Well, Mike the rooster did. Back in 1945, Farmer Lloyd Olsen decided it was time for Mike to take his place on the dinner table, so he took a swing at Mike with an axe. Like most chickens, Mike continued to move around after his head had been chopped off, but unlike all other chickens, he survived for nearly two years. It turns out that the blow had left Mike's brain stem intact, and as long as Farmer Olsen fed and watered him with an eyedropper, Mike could continue as normal. Except that as a live, headless chicken, he became a celebrity. People came to **Fruita, Colorado,** and paid Farmer Olsen a quarter a visit to look at the creature. He went on tour, too, through Atlantic City, New York, Los Angeles, and San Diego. But he did eventually die in 1947. Today, Fruita celebrates Mike the Headless Chicken Day in late May. And as they say in town: next time life gets you down, remember that you can live a normal life even after you've lost your mind!

Now where did I put that head?

Check it out!
www.miketheheadlesschicken.org

Here I am!

Roadkill Cook-off

When the great state of West Virginia passed a law allowing people to gather dead critters from the side of the road to use as food, the good people of Pocahontas County got a great idea. Why not hold an annual roadkill cook-off? Why not, indeed! Every September since that fateful day, residents from every corner of the county meet to show off their best recipes. This could only happen in the Weird U.S.—and we're glad it does. But we'll probably pass on the armadillo tacos and smeared hot hog with groundhog gravy!

Check it out!
www.pccocwy.com

The Bonnie & Clyde Festival

As far as bad guys go, Bonnie Parker and Clyde Barrow were probably the most notorious and infamous. During the early 1930s, they led a small gang in bank robberies and daring getaways in small towns across the South and West. Along the way, they killed a dozen people, including nine police officers. They came to a fitting end on May 23, 1934, when Texas and Louisiana authorities ambushed and killed them. This may not sound like a street fair waiting to happen, but each year in **Gibsland, Louisiana** (where the couple ate their last meal), residents throw a big shindig celebrating the couples' death. The festival features two reenactments: one of a bank robbery and the other of the ambush (held at the actual site)—fake bullets and blood and more! If you head to Gibsland, you can also visit the town's two museums dedicated to Bonnie and Clyde.

Gibsland, Louisiana is a great place to visit ... just don't get caught in the crossfire!

A WORLD OF THEIR OWN

Chapter **3**

how would you like to have the weirdest house in the neighborhood—the one that makes everyone stop and stare and sometimes laugh out loud? Well, if that's the kind of house you want, you're not alone. All over the country, there are people who have transformed their homes into eye-popping wonderlands, often using anything they can get their hands on, like aluminum cans, bottles, bicycle wheels, and even pieces of baby dolls. Sometimes the results are crazy and beautiful, and sometimes . . . uh, maybe just crazy. But these masterpieces are never, ever boring. Take a tour of "Weirder Homes and Gardens" and see for yourself. Maybe you'll get some strange decorating ideas of your own.

Now THAT'S what we call aluminum siding!

Aluminum (Can) Siding

Some artists are inspired by books, paintings, or movies. Richard Van Os Keuls was inspired when he saw a truck run over an empty soda can. He decided that the crushed can would make a perfect shingle. And so, when it came time to put aluminum siding on the new addition to his house in **Silver Spring, Maryland**, he came up with a very "canny" idea. That's right! He decided to shingle his house with his empties. After all, aluminum cans are cheap! They're colorful! And they're everywhere!

More than ten years and 20,000 cans later, he's still working on the project. Why is it taking so long? For one thing, rather than pouring out perfectly good soda, Van Os Keuls prefers to drink the contents of his cans before tacking them up. He also puts a lot of thought into where each can goes, making sure to separate his colors. The result is a magical rainbow-colored house that glitters in the sunshine. His idea may not be practical, and drinking so much soda is probably not very healthy, but no one who sees the aluminum-can-covered house can deny that Richard Van Os Keuls has come up with a beautiful twist on recycling.

Check it out!
www.philadelphiasmagicgardens.org

Philadelphia's Magic Gardens

"Art is the center of the real world."

You'll find this sentence repeated again and again in the Magic Gardens on South Street in **Philadelphia, Pennsylvania**. You'll also find weird sculptures of concrete mixed with broken statues, fan blades, bricks, bottles, bicycle wheels, and other assorted bric-a-brac. You might even be lucky enough to spot a sloppily dressed man with a long gray beard. He's the creator of this fascinating mishmash, a wildly imaginative artist named Isaiah Zagar. And if you do see him, try not to be put off by his strange appearance. He may be eccentric, but he's approachable.

Isaiah Zagar first arrived in Philadelphia in the late 1960s. Back then, Magic Gardens was a vacant lot, and South Street was a dangerous place with its boarded-up buildings and high crime rate. The artist stuck around because he thought that the location was perfect for his work. Today, the neighborhood is safe, and many people in Philadelphia believe that Mr. Zagar's beautiful artwork helped make it that way.

The Watts Towers

In 1921, Simon Rodia bought a little piece of land in the **Watts district of South Los Angeles, California**. Over the next thirty-three years, without any heavy machinery, he built towers that shot up almost a hundred feet into the sky. The only help he received was from neighborhood kids. He paid them pennies and they provided bottles, broken tiles, metal, pottery, marbles, mirrors, seashells, and anything else he could use to decorate his creation. He called it *Nuestro Pueblo*, which means "Our Town" in Spanish. "I had in my mind to do something big and I did it," he once said. He sure did! The Watts Towers have been called the single largest artwork ever created by one person.

Check it out!
www.wattstowers.us

The Forevertron

The Forevertron sits beside a junkyard five miles south of **Baraboo, Wisconsin**, on Highway 12. Weighing more than 300 tons, this scrap metal monstrosity features a recycled decontamination chamber from an old 1970s Apollo space mission. A mishmash of gears, springs, car parts, and electrical wiring surround a spiral staircase leading up to a glass egg encased in copper.

Ask around and you'll learn that the creator of this contraption is a mad genius named Dr. Evermor. His plan is a science-fiction fever dream: He hopes someday to climb the spiral staircase and sit inside the glass egg. Then, a bolt of lightning will strike and the Forevertron will harness its energy and send the good doctor hurtling into space. Dr. Evermor also hopes that the public will come to watch him blast off, so he's constructed a scrap-metal gazebo for refreshments as well as viewing stations.

By this point, you probably have a lot of questions. Who is Dr. Evermor? Is he as crazy as he sounds? Can I go for a ride in the lightning-powered egg, too? We asked the same questions when we recently visited the Forevertron and discovered that Dr. Evermor is actually Thomas O. Every, a man who retired from the scrap-metal recycling business in 1983. "I was an industrial wrecker for a great period of time, and we destroyed a lot of things," said Mr. Every. "It gets working on your psyche—tearing all this stuff down. I wanted to build something up instead."

With this in mind, Every invented the character of Dr. Evermor and created Dr. Evermor's Art Park, featuring the largest scrap-metal sculpture in the world, his masterpiece, the Forevertron. So it's all fantasy, Dr. Evermor and his lightning-powered Forevertron? Yes, but still we can't help hoping that the thing really works. After all, who knows? Maybe someday, Thomas O. Every will step out of his workshop in his Dr. Evermor suit and will climb the Forevertron and ride off into the heavens.

Coffeepot Houses vs. Teapot Houses

One morning at Weird Central, we decided to tackle an extremely important question: are there more houses shaped like coffeepots or teapots in the U.S.?

(Okay, so it seemed important to us at the time!)

"Coffeepots!" insisted the coffee drinkers among us.

"Teapots!" shouted the tea lovers.

"Coffeepots!"

"Teapots!"

It went on and on. Finally, to settle the issue and avoid an all-out war at Weird, we decided to have a contest: Coffeepot Houses vs. Teapot Houses!

This lovely two-story pot near **Bedford, Pennsylvania,** gave coffee an early lead. Originally built as a coffee shop in 1925, it's now the visitors' center for the town of Bedford.

Tea ties it up with the World's Largest Teapot in **Chester, West Virginia**. Built in 1938, this teapot has weathered rough times and come out tooting. Over the years, it's been used to sell root beer, pottery, souvenirs, and fast food.

Our research quickly uncovered another coffeepot house in **Lexington, Virginia**. Unfortunately, this big metal pot—complete with handle and spout—has seen better days. It was a restaurant from 1959 to the late 1970s, but today it's empty, and the last time we checked, a For Rent sign was displayed in the window.

Will coffee beat tea? Or will tea beat coffee? Will we ever stop this silliness and get some real work done? The argument continued for hours. The mysterious Kettle House in **Galveston, Texas**, was disqualified because it looked more like a huge Crock-Pot than a teakettle. We also rejected the House of Mugs in **Colletsville, North Carolina**. A house decorated with hundreds of coffee mugs is certainly an impressive sight. But a bunch of coffee mugs does not make a coffeepot house! So, we're calling it a tie! If you happen to stumble upon a house that looks oddly potlike, please let us know, because goofy contests like this are never meant to end. At least, not at Weird Central!

The Teapot Dome Gas Station in **Zillah, Washington**, evens the score.

The Mushroom House

The neighborhood looked perfectly normal—a suburb in **Bethesda, Maryland**, near Washington D.C. We were out in the Weirdmobile, checking out a story we'd heard about a strange house known as the Mushroom House. We passed rows and rows of houses. Some were a bit ugly, but not ugly like a mushroom. So we drove on. Then, we found it. We parked and studied the building before us. Everyone in the Weirdmobile was speechless. Finally, someone broke the silence. "A giant mushroom? I think it looks more like a big melting lump of ice cream." The owner stepped out. His name was Eddie Garfinkle, and he spoke excitedly about his weird home.

"Our heating and cooling bills are much lower than our friends' with much smaller houses," he told us. "It's like living in a big thermos." He explained that the Mushroom House was a 1922 farmhouse that was covered with spray-on insulating foam called polystucco. "We were looking for something economical and out of the ordinary." Mr. Garfinkle made it all sound so sane and practical that, for a moment, we considered dumping truckloads of polystucco on our own homes. In the end, we decided not to. It was fun to visit a house that looked like a gigantic mushroom (or a big glob of melting ice cream), but we weren't sure if were really wanted to live in one.

This time, you can't blame polystucco. This home in **Pittsford, New York**, was built by James H. Johnson, who set out to design a dwelling that looked like an umbrella-shaped flower called Queen Anne's Lace. We think that it turned out more funguslike than flowerlike. But in our weird world, that's not a bad thing.

Totem Pole Park

Here's one for you trivia buffs. Where can you find the world's largest concrete totem pole? Answer: Totem Pole Park in **Foyil, Oklahoma**. A tribute to Native Americans, the sixty-foot-tall totem pole is covered with colorful carved pictures. At the top are four American Indians, each symbolizing a different tribe. At the bottom is a concrete turtle with an uncomfortable look on its face. (If you were supporting a 134-ton totem pole, you wouldn't look so happy either!)

The enormous totem pole is the handiwork of Ed Galloway (1880–1962), a woodworking teacher who decided to build the pole to keep busy after retirement. The project took eleven years and, for the most part, he worked alone.

Totem Pole Park also features other creations by Ed Galloway, including smaller totem poles, totem-pole picnic tables, and a totem-pole fireplace. He even built a house made of totem poles. What do you think he put inside his eleven-sided totem-pole house? His collection of handmade fiddles. What did you expect, more totem poles?

A Whirlwind Whirligig Tour

In the world of weird yard art, there's one particular decoration that we've seen again and again. Can you guess what it is? Scrap-metal dinosaurs? Bowling-ball pyramids? Giant cement heads? Yes, we've seen all of those. But, according to our exhaustive research, one of the most popular weird lawn objects is the whirligig. What's a whirligig? Something that whirls in the wind, of course! A windmill is a whirligig. So is a weather vane. And if you taped pinwheels to your arms and legs and stood outside, facing the wind, then you'd be a whirligig (and please send pictures if you decide to try this out).

Emil Gehrke loved making windmills, and he especially loved experimenting, using different kinds of weird objects to catch the wind—things such as spoons and plates, hard hats, funnels, pots, and pie tins. Mr. Gehrke died in 1979, but his wonderful collection of windmills is still displayed on tall poles in a park not far from Grand Coulee Dam, in **Electric City, Washington**.

Herron Briggs of **Greenville, South Carolina**, specialized in a particular kind of whirligig. He made colorful, eye-popping, wind-catching airplanes. He built his flying machines using blades from old electric fans (for propellers) and a variety of other things he found around the house—pipes, tin cans, and lawn-mower wheels. Before he passed away in 1999, people would flock from all over to see Herron Briggs' yard full of earthbound airplanes. Eventually, they started calling him the Whirligig Man.

Vollis Simpson didn't have art in mind when he built his first whirligig. In World War II, stationed on the Mariana Islands, he built one to power a washing machine. Today, his farm in **Lucama, North Carolina** is a hotspot for whirligig lovers around the world. Some of his whirli-gigantic creations are more than fifty feet tall, and most are covered with reflectors, so, on windy days, they sparkle and gleam in the sunlight as they twirl. Vollis Simpson's scrap-metal whirligigs became so famous that four of them were displayed in Atlanta, Georgia, for the 1996 Olympic Games.

Once a year, Whirligig-mania comes to the town of **Wilson, North Carolina**. Inspired by the work of Vollis Simpson, Wilson holds its annual Whirligig Festival in the first week of November. The event, which draws thousands of spectators, includes a whirligig contest, a class on whirligig making, and whirligig vendors selling their wind-powered wares.

These whirligigs light up at night!

Check it out!
www.wilsonwhirligigfestival.com

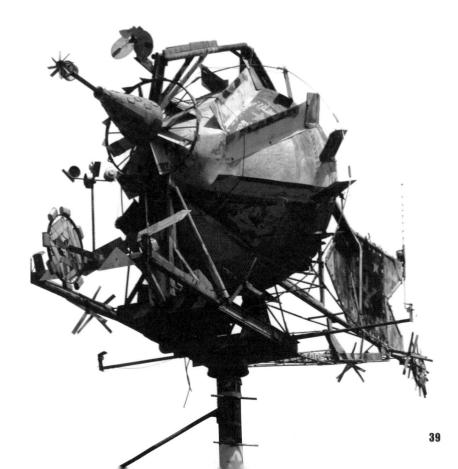

Bishop's Castle

Jim Bishop didn't set out to construct a castle. The project started out as a one-room cottage in **Wetmore, Colorado**. But like most people in this chapter, Mr. Bishop couldn't stop building. Obsessively, he kept adding to the structure, making towers and ballrooms, single-handedly moving more than a thousand tons of rocks in the process. He calls his castle a place "where dreams happen." To prove it, he built a fire-breathing dragon and placed it near the top. His creation is considered the biggest one-man construction job in the United States. And, as far as we know, he's still building.

Check it out! www.bishopcastle.info

Petersen Rock Garden

If you enjoy rock collecting, or if you enjoy taking road trips to really cool places, then you should definitely visit the Petersen Rock Garden and Museum in **Redmond, Oregon**. Rasmus Petersen (1883–1952) loved roaming around, collecting all kinds of colorful rocks—obsidian, petrified wood, malachite, and thunder eggs. When he got home, he'd build things with them. Using mortar, little shards of glass, and piles and piles of rocks, he made bridges and castles. And to express his love for America, he made his own Statue of Liberty, a miniature Independence Hall, and an American flag—all out of stones. The rock gardens are still maintained by the Petersen family and are open to the public.

Prairie Moon Museum and Sculpture Garden

Herman Rusch was a farmer until he stopped working in 1952. To stay active in his retirement, he decided to convert the Prairie Moon Dance Pavilion in **Cochrane, Wisconsin**, into a museum. He proceeded to fill the museum with all sorts of curiosities. One example: a washing machine powered by a goat on a treadmill. Then, he began sprucing up the grounds of the museum. And that's when things really began to get weird. He made a Hindu temple, concrete dinosaurs, a giant frowning bust of himself, and a spectacular fence that has to be seen to be believed. It looks kind of like fantasyland created by a dessert chef: giant colorful ice-cream cones connected by arches on top of arches, holding sprinkles and oversized chocolate chips. Who could have imagined that a fence could look so, um, edible?

Check it out!
www.bottlevillage.com

Grandma Prisbrey's Bottle Village

If you can shingle a house with aluminum cans, why not make a whole village out of bottles? That's what an eccentric woman did in her yard in **Simi Valley, California**. It all started in 1956 because sixty-year-old Grandma Prisbrey had a large collection of pencils. Eventually, her collection hit the 17,000 pencil mark! She needed a place to keep them, so she decided to build a pencil house. To keep it cheap, she used mortar and old bottles that she found at the dump. Unfortunately, she also found a lot of other stuff that she liked at the dump. But where was she going to put it? Obviously, she had to build more bottle houses. She continued building for thirty-five years, making wishing wells, tiled paths, a playhouse for her grandchildren called the Rumpus Room, and strange creations like the Leaning Tower of Bottle Village and Dolls Head Shrine. And the best part was that for a quarter, she'd give you a guided tour!

Sadly, Grandma Prisbrey died in 1988, and in 1994, an earthquake nearly destroyed Bottle Village. The damage was so serious that these days you can see the village only in books and on the Internet. But there's hope! A group called P.B.V. (Preserve Bottle Village) is raising money for repairs. Maybe, with their help, you'll soon be able to take a tour through Grandma Prisbrey's Bottle Village so you can see for yourself how weird and wonderful it is.

ROADSIDE ODDITIES

imagine that your family is driving down the road and you pass a giant house shaped like a shoe. Would you:
A) Get excited and ask your parents to stop?
B) Ignore it (life's too short to pay attention to giant shoe houses)?

If you answered "A," you have what we like to call "the Weird Eye."

If you have the Weird Eye, every car ride has the potential to be a wild adventure full of jaw-dropping discoveries and head-scratching whatsits. There are far too many roadside oddities in America for us to even scratch the surface. But to give you something to gawk at, we've gathered together some of our favorites.

Ocean City, Maryland
Don't let the eye-patch and pirate hat fool you! The giant pirate at the entrance to the Jolly Roger Amusement Park is actually a Muffler Man.
(You can tell by the way he's holding his sword.)

Invasion of the Muffler Men

The Muffler Men are everywhere! You just have to know how to spot them. A typical Muffler Man stands more than twenty feet tall and is made of fiberglass. He looks friendly and strong, and most often wears an open-necked, short-sleeve shirt. But the most distinguishing characteristic of a Muffler Man is the position of his hands—his left hand always faces up and his right hand always faces down. This pose makes it easy for Muffler Men to hold things . . . such as mufflers, for example.

However, the first Muffler Man was designed to carry an axe. Made by Prewitt Fiberglass in 1962, he was modeled after the legendary lumberjack Paul Bunyan, and stood before the PB Café on Route 66 in **Flagstaff, Arizona**. Prewitt Fiberglass became International Fiberglass, and the company began churning out roadside giants using the Paul Bunyan mold over and over again. They sold their creations to all kinds of businesses across the country. Restaurants often turned the gentle giant into an oversized chef carrying a rolling pin. And auto-repair shops gave him a muffler. That's how the Muffler Man got his name. The Muffler Men are still among us. Sometimes they're hard to recognize. You have to learn to see through their disguises.

Someone stole my muffler and left me with this hot dog!

I need new pants.

Atlanta, Illinois
The Hot Dog Muffler Man in front of Bunyon's Restaurant in Cicero was famous to drivers familiar with Route 66. The statue was so popular that, after Bunyon's closed, the Muffler Man was moved to the town square of Atlanta.

Wilmington, Illinois
Blast off! The Gemini Giant wears an astronaut suit. But instead of riding in a rocket ship, he's carrying one. The giant space explorer stands guard over the Launching Pad Drive-in.

Havre de Grace, Maryland
This small harbor town is known for having a very impressive Muffler Man that sports soldier's fatigues.

Newport News, Virginia
The Auto Muffler King! A classic Muffler Man, holding up a muffler on Jefferson Avenue. Someone tell the owner that his pants need a new paint job!

Unger, Land of the Giants

You probably know a few people who have garden gnomes or pink flamingoes on their front lawn, but we bet you don't know anybody with a giant Santa and four even bigger giants on their driveway. We do. They're George and Pam Farnham, and they live in **Unger, West Virginia**. From the long and winding road that leads to their farm, you can see a looming Santa, a lumberjack, a boy with grocery bags, a bikini-wearing lady, and a twenty-foot surfer—all in a row. George has been collecting regular garden statues for years, but when his wife bought him a special giant one for his birthday, he took the idea and ran with it.

Check it out!
www.fastkorp.com

Want your own fiberglass giant? Check out the FAST Corporation headquarters in **Sparta, Wisconsin**. FAST Corporation stands for Fiberglass Animals, Shapes & Trademarks Corporation, and if you want something big made out of fiberglass, FAST Corporation is the place to go. Fiberglass bicycle-riding giants, dinosaurs, cows, sharks, and rhinos. FAST Corporation makes them all, and they display their latest masterpieces out on the lawn. The outdoor showroom is always changing, so when you visit you never know what you might see.

Check it out!
www.shoehouse.us

Haines Shoe House

Route 30 is a major road that leads through the lower part of **Pennsylvania**. How boring does that sound? Well, before you fall asleep, keep your eyes open for the Shoe House between **York** and **Lancaster**. Back in 1948, the area's most successful shoe salesman, a fellow called Mahlon Haines, built a three-story house in the shape of his favorite footwear. Back in the day, Mr. Haines' customers could stay there for free for a weekend—all they had to do was ask at one of his stores and he'd book them in. These days, it's open to the public from June through August and on the weekends in the spring and fall.

The Awakening

To look at this snapshot taken at the **National Harbor in Maryland**, you would think that a buried giant is struggling to break free. His right arm and left leg are thrusting up from the ground. It's only a matter of time before he's out and about and wreaking havoc in our nation's capital. Run away!

Oops. False alarm. The aluminum giant is a monstrous statue—actually five statues—created by sculptor J. Seward Johnson, Jr.

WORLD'S LARGEST PEANUT

The World's Biggest and Smallest

If you travel across the country with your Weird Radar buzzing, you're sure to notice a large number of fiberglass cows. You might even wonder which is the biggest. And if you're stuck in traffic with a lot of time on your hands, you might come up with some other silly questions, such as, "Where is the world's shortest street?" "Where is the world's tiniest park?" "How long am I going to be stuck in this stupid traffic jam?"

We can't help you with that last one, but we have answers to the others. Here are some of the biggest and smallest sites to visit as you inch your way across Weird America.

The World's Biggest Peanut

There's a sign in **Durant, Oklahoma**, that points you toward the Big Peanut. And this nut is certainly amazing, but at three feet, it's about seven feet short of the world's record.

Georgia is famous for peanut farming, so it makes sense that the world's largest peanut would be found there. Ten feet tall, it rests on top of a fifteen-foot pedestal in Ashburn, and it's surrounded by a gold crown that bears the message, "Georgia—1st in Peanuts."

Another town that's first in peanuts is **Peanut, Pennsylvania** (not to be confused with other Pennsylvania towns such as Upper Peanut and Lower Peanut). The town of Peanut doesn't have the world's biggest peanut, but it was the site of one of the biggest events in peanut history. On November 6, 1993, a group of peanut lovers in Peanut made the world's biggest peanut butter and jelly sandwich. They used 150 pounds of peanut butter and fifty pounds of jelly to make a sandwich that was nearly forty feet long.

GEORGIA 1ST in PEANUTS

The World's Shortest Street

"McKinley St.—World's Shortest Street" says the sign in **Bellefontaine, Ohio**. And McKinley Street is only about fifteen feet long, so you might not think to doubt Bellefontaine's claim. Except, according to the *Guinness Book of World Records*, the world's shortest street is Ebenezer Place in Wick, Scotland. This tiny Scottish road measures only 6 feet, 9 inches (which means that it's only five inches longer than Abe Lincoln lying down).

Too bad for Bellefontaine. They'll have to change their sign to read, "McKinley St.—World's Second Shortest Street."

The World's Largest Cow

Unless we hear of a bigger fiberglass cow somewhere in Scotland, the world's biggest bovine is Salem Sue in **New Salem, North Dakota**. And what a sight to behold! The docile creature stands thirty-eight-feet tall and is fifty feet long. Perched on a grassy field on School Hill, she can be seen for miles. In fact, you can spot Salem Sue from I-94 about two hours west of Jamestown, which is home to the world's largest cement buffalo!

The World's Largest Basket

For years, the Longaberger Basket Company in **Newark, Ohio**, was known only for making normal-sized baskets. Then Dave Longaberger started thinking big. He built a twenty-foot-tall picnic basket. Soon after, he outdid himself by creating the World's Largest Apple Basket, full of monstrous apples. It's in Frazeysburg, Ohio, and it's just under thirty feet tall. But before he died in 1999, Dave Longaberger produced his masterpiece. The Longaberger Basket Building is an exact copy of the Longaberger Medium Market Basket, only 160 times bigger!

Seven stories tall, the building is the workplace of five hundred employees. Maybe someday, another basket tycoon will come along and build a basket-shaped skyscraper, but until then, the Longaberger Basket Building is the basket to end all baskets!

The World's Smallest Park

Mill Ends Park is so small that no one can stroll in it. It's a two-foot-wide circle located in a traffic median on SW Naito Parkway in **Portland, Oregon**. The park was the idea of newspaperman Dick Fagan. On St. Patrick's Day 1948, Fagan decided that the location was ideal for snail races and leprechaun colonies. Since then, Portland residents have been adding whimsical touches of their own—a swimming pool for butterflies with a tiny diving board and a miniature Ferris wheel.

World's Largest Tennis Ball Tree

Okay, we're cheating here—this is the *only* tennis ball tree that we know of, but it sure is big. Driving through the desert in Utah, you might spot this oddity: a ninety-foot-tall tree sprouting multicolored tennis balls. Huge pieces of tennis balls lay scattered on the ground nearby like fallen leaves. Don't worry. It's not a desert mirage. It's a work of art by Swedish artist Karl Momen. But wouldn't it be cool if tennis balls actually did grow on trees?

The World's Largest Globe

The pride and joy of the DeLorme Map Store in **Yarmouth, Maine**, is Eartha, a globe that reaches three stories high. The dimensions of Eartha are truly spectacular. She's forty-one-feet tall, has a circumference of 130 feet and weighs 5,600 pounds. And like the Earth, she rotates on an axis tilted at 23.5 degrees. Eartha was created in 1998 by David DeLorme, the store's owner. He set out to build the largest printed image of the Earth in history and he succeeded tremendously. The only terrestrial globe bigger than Eartha is the world itself.

Check it out!
www.delorme.com

The World's Largest Ball of Twine

Where can you find the world's biggest ball of twine? Well, it's sort of complicated. The answer might be **Cawker City, Kansas**. Or it might be **Darwin, Minnesota**. These two towns have been fighting over the world record for years.

I'm bigger than you are!

The story began in 1950 when Francis Johnson started hand rolling a ball of twine in Darwin. Three years later, Frank Stoeber of Cawker City began a ball of his own. The two twine-rolling titans battled it out for years. Stoeber had the title of world's largest from the late fifties until he died in 1974. With his opponent out of the picture, Francis Johnson quickly caught up and brought the title back to Minnesota. Not to be outdone, Cawker City residents banded together to add to Stoeber's twine ball until it, once again, beat out the Darwin ball.

The Darwinian's insist that the Cawker City ball should be disqualified because it's not the work of a single person. Besides, they point out that the Cawker City ball isn't even ball shaped. It's saggy like a big leaky basketball, whereas the Darwin ball is a perfect sphere.

So . . . where is the world's biggest ball of twine? Darwin, Minnesota? Nope. Cawker City, Kansas? Wrong again! According to the *Guinness World Records*, the world's biggest ball of twine is in **Branson, Missouri**. It was built by a millionaire named J. C. Payne, and it took him only four years because he used a system of pulleys.

No you're knot!

A Giant Junk-Food Journey

Hungry? Let's go on a giant food road trip!

Let's start our voyage in **Los Angeles, California**, where we can stop for wieners at Tail o' the Pup, the city's famous hot-dog-shaped hot-dog joint.

Want something sweet? Sample some of Randy's Donuts (also in **Los Angeles**). The giant cement donut sitting on the shop looks heavy enough to crush the place, but somehow Randy's has survived for more than fifty years.

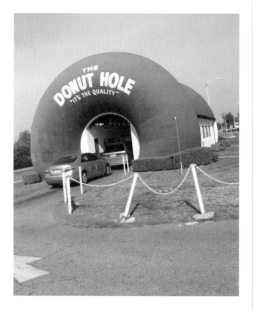

What? More donuts?! Let's try the Donut Hole in **La Puente, California**. This drive-through donuttery is flanked by two massive fiberglass pastries. The sign on the place says, "It's the Quality," but there's a lot of novelty to enjoy at the Donut Hole as well.

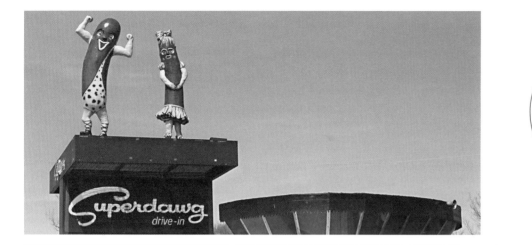

And our first-place wiener is ...

What's with all the hot dogs? The Superdawg Drive-in in **Chicago, Illinois**, features two giant hot dogs fastened to the roof—a boy and a girl.

How about something besides hot dogs and donuts? In **Marietta, Georgia**, you can eat your KFC next to a fifty-six-foot-tall steel chicken.

Let's enjoy one last treat at Twistee Treat in **Kissimmee, Florida**.

By now your belly must be aching, your fingers sticky, and your car smelling like a dumpster outside a fast-food restaurant. It's time to call it quits and head back home. Perhaps we've all bitten off more than we could chew.

Porter Sculpture Park

The sixty-foot-tall bull's head is visible for miles, but it's only one of the many amazing sculptures to see at the Porter Sculpture Park in **Montrose, South Dakota**. There's a creepy jack-in-the-box waving a spiked club, a gargantuan yellow steel hand with a butterfly perched on its finger, dinosaur skeletons, oversized goldfish, and lots more. If you take a road trip to the Porter Sculpture Park, you might even meet Wayne Porter, the artist behind it all. And if you're lucky, he'll give you a guided tour and tell you what he was thinking when he made all of this weirdness.

Check it out!
www.portersculpturepark.com

What's That Doing Here?

Some vacationers who visit the Eiffel Tower in France come back with snapshots and souvenirs. More ambitious tourists return with their heads full of dreams. And as soon as they get home, they make these dreams come true by building Eiffel Towers of their own. Perhaps this is why there are eight replicas of the Eiffel Tower in the United States. We'd like to pay a Weird tribute to these obsessive copycats. If it weren't for them, we'd never have the enjoyable experience of spotting world landmarks in odd locations where they're not supposed to be.

The Eiffel Tower of Paris, Texas

Well, the town is called Paris. Why shouldn't it have its own Eiffel Tower? Next to the real Eiffel Tower, this reproduction might not be so impressive. It's only sixty-five-feet tall and the real one is about a thousand feet taller! In the spectrum of imitation Eiffel Towers around the world (there are fifteen that we know of), the copy in Texas falls, size wise, somewhere in the middle. But it has something that the other replicas lack—a cowboy hat!

The Leaning Tower of Pisa Niles

It's half the size of the Leaning Tower of Pisa, but it's closer. The city of **Niles, Illinois**, constructed its leaning tower clone in 1934. Originally designed as a water tower, it was the object of ridicule when it was finished. Local residents called it Farr's Folly (after the tower's architect, Albert Farr). In time, public opinion softened, and now the Leaning Tower of Niles is the centerpiece of a park and a popular attraction.

In an interview about the McRae Statue of Liberty, Lion Ray Bowers said, "We never knew it would be so pretty."

Statues of Liberty

The Statue of Liberty in New York City harbor turned 100 in 1986. And in honor of her birthday, there was a brief wave of Statue-of-Liberty-copycat-mania around the country.

An artist named Gene Stilp created a scaled-down version and placed it on a railway bridge piling in the middle of the Susquehanna River near **Dauphin, Pennsylvania**. No match for bad weather, the statue was soon gone. With the support of the town, Stilp set out to build a more durable, fake Statue of Liberty. The new lady is held in place by cables, so she should stay put for a while.

Georgia's Statue of Liberty was made by the Lion's Club of McRae. Her head is a tree stump. Her hand is a glove stuffed with concrete. Green paint. Styrofoam. Fiberglass-coated sheets. The Lion's Club members used whatever they could find. When they were finished, their creation received more attention than they ever imagined.

Stonehenge II, III, IV, Etc.

The Eiffel Tower . . . The Leaning Tower of Pisa . . . What other European landmarks are there left to remake? How about Stonehenge? Of course, replicas of Stonehenge don't carry the mystery of the original megalith in England. The only mysterious aspect of America's copycat Stonehenges is why there are so many of them.

Stonehenge II is a strange site that had a strange beginning. Al Shepperd received a huge limestone slab for his birthday. He stood it up in a field that he owned in **Hunt, Texas**, and he liked what he saw. So he and a friend, Doug Hill, put some money together to buy some more slabs. They ended up with a full reproduction of Stonehenge as well as a couple giant fake Easter Island heads.

Dum-Dum want gum gum.

We don't know whether or not Al wanted a huge limestone slab for his birthday, but we're sure glad he got one!

Foamhenge in **Natural Bridge, Virginia**, is made of Styrofoam. Mark Cline, the creator of the lightweight monument, decided to anchor the "stones" in concrete. Otherwise, they might blow down the highway and cause all sorts of chaos.

Carhenge in **Alliance, Nebraska**, and Stonefridge in **Santa Fe, New Mexico**, carry on the grand tradition of Stonehenge rip-offs. Using cars and refrigerators to replicate Stonehenge, these artworks provoke wonder and laughter alike. Inspired by them, we've come up with some ideas for mock-Stonehenges of our own: Hedgehenge! Legohenge! Port-a-potty-henge! Muffler-man-henge! If there's a –henge you'd like to see, let us know about it. Or better yet, find an open field and just start building!

Cars on a Spike

You won't be taking any "Huh?" pictures of the Spindle in **Berwyn, Illinois**, because the artwork by Dustin Shuler was dismantled in 2008 to make room for a Walgreens. The sculpture—a tower of eight cars skewered on a giant spike—was loved by many and viewed as an eyesore by a few. In a desperate move, the sculpture was posted on eBay, but no one matched the starting bid of $50,000. Now, "Cars on a Spike" joins a long list of roadside oddities that exist in fond memories and photos. We'll miss the rusty attraction, but we're sure that as long as there are cars, weird artists will continue to make weird sculptures with them.

Booger Hollow Double-Decker Outhouse

The images conjured up by the phrase "double-decker outhouse" are not particularly pleasant. And if you're wondering how to solve the obvious problems associated with multitiered waste facilities, then you're not alone. In fact, the double-decker outhouse in **Pope County, Arkansas**, hasn't figured out a solution either. There's a jokey sign out front, which says, "Upstairs closed 'til we figur out plummin."

The two-story outhouse used to be the restroom for the Booger Hollow Trading Post. But Booger Hollow has fallen on hard times. According to the town's welcome sign, the town has "Population 7 Counten' One Coon Dog." Unfortunately, this estimate is overly optimistic. Since the trading post was sold in 2004, the town has been abandoned.

A ghost town with a double-decker outhouse! It's so absurd that somehow it seems perfectly logical. At least, to us.

What do you mean you can't find a spot?
Park on top of the Bug!

This place is a kick in the pants!

I Could Have Kicked Myself

Have you ever said, "I want to kick myself"? Well, here's your chance. These words are posted on a sign behind the Angus Barn Restaurant near the **Raleigh-Durham airport in North Carolina**. The sign also lists the rules for using the restaurant's "I Want to Kick Myself" machine.

Nothing could be simpler. You bend over and turn a crank. Then, the boots behind you start spinning and . . . ouch! Pay special attention to Rule #5: The Angus Barn will not be responsible for anyone who does not like the way they were kicked."

Surprisingly, there's another "I Want to Kick Myself" machine about three hours away in the town of Croatan, which leads to the question . . . What is it about North Carolina that makes people want to kick themselves?

HAVE YOU EVER SAID "I WANT TO KICK MYSELF" HERES YOUR CHANCE

RULES

1. USE MACHINE AT OWN RISK
2. CHILDREN UNDER 12 MUST BE SUPERVISED BY AN ADULT
3. ONE PERSON AT A TIME PLEASE
4. DO NOT STAND FACING BOOTS
5. THE ANGUS BARN WILL NOT BE RESPONSIBLE FOR ANYONE WHO DOES NOT LIKE THE WAY THEY WERE KICKED

The Neon Boneyard and the Neon Museum

The signs in the Neon Boneyard in **Las Vegas, Nevada**, have certainly seen brighter days. They're no longer colorful, no longer flashing, and the establishments they advertise have been closed for years. Yet, even turned off, these broken-down neon signs are still fascinating.

Fortunately, an organization is trying to save old neon signs. It's pulling them from the Neon Boneyard, repairing them, and installing them in the Neon Museum on Fremont Street. A giant cowboy riding a light-studded horse. An enormous, sparkling neon Aladdin's lamp from the world famous Aladdin Hotel. Beaming signs for restaurants and wedding chapels. The Neon Museum has an eye-popping collection of neon fixer-uppers, bright and flashy blasts from Las Vegas's past.

Check it out!
www.neonmuseum.org

HAUNTED HOLIDAY

a s we huddle around the campfire outside of Weird Central making s'mores and watching the shadows flicker in the darkness, we know that it won't be long before someone tells a ghost story. The night just wouldn't be the same without one. You can't beat the tingling sensation of a well-told ghost story. Of course, the best ones happen in places we know or involve people we've met. And we have heard many of them over the years. So, we're proud—and a little scared—to present the freakiest part of our freaky road trip: haunted houses, roads, bridges, and even stores.

The Winchester Mystery House

Of all the strange houses that we've seen (and believe me, we've seen plenty!), perhaps the spookiest and most perplexing is the Winchester Mystery House in **San Jose, California**. The woman behind this amazing house was named Sarah Winchester. To say that

Um . . . I was looking for the restroom.

she was eccentric is an understatement. To start with, she was a *triskaidekaphile*, which is just a complicated way of saying that Sarah Winchester loved the number 13. Sarah was married to William Wirt Winchester, whose family was ridiculously wealthy because his father's company made the Winchester repeating rifle. Filled with grief over the death of her daughter and, later, her husband's death, an inconsolable Sarah visited a psychic who told her that these unfortunate events were linked to the Winchester rifle, which had taken countless lives. The spirits of the dead were angry and now sought revenge on the Winchester family! Yet, the psychic insisted that there was hope. Sarah was instructed to move West, where she would spend the cursed Winchester fortune by building a house. The house would need to be huge to provide plenty of room for friendly spirits, and it also needed to be elaborate and confusing so vengeful ghosts would get lost trying to find Sarah.

Sarah did as she was told. In 1884, she purchased a farmhouse in San Jose. Then, she began transforming it into one of the weirdest mansions ever. The remodeling lasted thirty-eight years and went on twenty-four hours a day, seven days a week. Sarah never used plans or blueprints and she never consulted with an architect. Instead, she received advice from the Great Beyond during nightly séances. During these ghostly encounters, she would find out what to build or tear down the following day.

Six hundred rooms with ten thousand windows were installed, as well as two ballrooms, six kitchens, and forty bedrooms. With so many bedrooms to choose from, Sarah started sleeping in a different one every night. Often, the spirit communications led to bizarre constructions such as false passageways, windows in floors, doors opening into walls, tiny doorways, and tiny hallways. There are also stairs leading to a dead end at the ceiling, stairs that head down and then back up (serving no purpose), and winding stairs that go on and on but barely rise. On the day Sarah Winchester died, the workmen simply stopped working, leaving nails protruding from walls and sections of the house half-built. It remains, to this day, a magnificent, unfinished, meandering maze. There are rumors that, if you visit the Winchester Mystery House, you might spot Sarah's ghost wandering around the premises. Maybe, even after her death, she's still considering remodeling.

Check it out!

www.winchestermysteryhouse.com

One night in August 1976, a driver noticed a girl inside the gates of Resurrection Cemetery, clutching the bars as she looked out to the street. He stopped by the police station to say someone had been locked in the cemetery. The officer who investigated found the bars of the gate were bent, broken, and scorched by an intense heat . . . and upon them were small handprints. Some people believe it was Resurrection Mary!

Dancing with Death

When Jerry Palus asked a pretty girl to dance with him at **Chicago's** Liberty Grove Hall, he had no idea he would become part of the most famous ghost story in the area. The dance took place way back in 1939, but people at newspapers and on TV would ask him about that night right up until he died, more than fifty years later. So what happened?

The girl said her name was Mary, and they chatted and danced for a while. She gave Jerry her address. Eventually, he offered to drive her home. He had noticed as they danced that her hands were very cold and her mind seemed to be distracted, but otherwise, Mary seemed like a nice girl. It was on the drive back when things got strange. She asked him to drive north along Archer Avenue. This seemed like the wrong way to her house, but Mary insisted. When they reached the Resurrection Cemetery, she told Jerry to stop the car to let her out. Jerry was confused, but he offered to walk her across the road. She turned to him and said quietly, "This is where I have to get out. Where I'm going, you can't follow." And she dashed out of the car toward the cemetery gates.

As Jerry watched her go, she disappeared right before his eyes. Jerry still had Mary's home address, so he visited the next day, only to find out Mary had died years earlier. She was struck by a car and killed after an evening of dancing at the nearby Willowbrook. Her mother showed Jerry some family photographs, and sure enough, he recognized the girl he had danced with in one of them. Even before the night she danced with Jerry Palus, Resurrection Mary was often seen along Archer Avenue on the road to Resurrection Cemetery. And she still shows up to this day.

Lydia

It's hard to imagine a creepier bridge along an old back road than this one in **North Carolina**, between Greensboro and Jamestown. Underneath the main railroad is an old, narrow tunnel, overgrown with weeds. Many years ago, this was part of the main route between the two towns, and it's the place where many young men found a sad-looking girl named Lydia, standing alone in a party dress. The men would gallantly offer her a ride and hear the tale of how she had been at a party in Raleigh with friends and left in anger after an argument. She needed to get home to High Point, and she was tired and lost. So the young men would drive her to her door.

This story was first told in the 1920s, so the young men showed a courtesy you don't often see nowadays—they would get out of the driver's side door and walk around to the other side to open the door for their passenger. And when they did, they would find Lydia's seat empty. They would assume she had slipped out of the car and would go to the front door of the house to make sure she had arrived safely. When they did, Lydia's mother would tell them something they did not expect:

"Lydia never comes home. She was killed on that road. Almost every night, someone like you tries to bring her back here. As soon as they pull into the drive, she's gone again . . . gone to spend another cold night out by the road."

They say that Lydia still hikes along High Point Road. Sometimes they say she's stuck under the old overgrown tunnel where nobody drives anymore.

Check it out! www.thelodgeresort.com

Rebecca Roams the Cloudcroft Lodge

If you ever visit The Lodge in **Cloudcroft, New Mexico,** say hi to Rebecca. She's been staying at this hotel for more than a hundred years. She has long red hair, an easy smile, and a good sense of humor. Oh, yeah, she's also a ghost. One hot spot of strange signs is Room 101, the Governor's Suite. The phone on the front desk often gets phone calls from Room 101 even when the room is empty. The light in the ceiling fan just outside of Room 101 turns off and on at will.

Grant Park's Seven Bridges

If you want to freak yourself out, some people say you should take an evening stroll through Seven Bridges in Grant Park on the south side of **Milwaukee, Wisconsin**. If the moon is full, you may see colored lights dancing around in the woods. If you walk toward the lights, you'll then hear laughter, screams, footsteps, and even heavy breathing. If you let the footsteps get closer, an incredibly uneasy feeling will creep over you. Legend has it that many people had been killed here and that their murderers later committed suicide in the park. It's also rumored that if you stand on one of the bridges, a mist or an apparition will appear right in front of you. The apparition is most likely one of the murder victims.

Beware the Lights of the Hookerman!

What could be creepier than the sight of mysterious lights appearing on an abandoned railroad track, moving toward you at great speed? You know it's not a train—they haven't run on this track for years. Besides, the light bobs, sways, and glows with different colors. It's nothing like a train light. No, this is the Hookerman's light, and people have been going to three sites in **New Jersey** to see it for nearly a hundred years.

The legend of the Hookerman explains the lights like this: A railroad worker was working on the tracks many years ago, when a train ran into him and damaged his arm so badly the doctors replaced his hand with a hook. Some say the accident drove him mad, and he spent the rest of his life in a hospital. When he died, his spirit began to wander the track looking for his lost arm, carrying a lantern that swings on his hook. You can imagine how creepy it is when you're at one of the three Hookerman sites— Four Bridges Road in Flanders, Naugherton Road in Washington Township, or Roycefield Road in Hillsborough—and you actually see the light appear. It really does, too. Lots of people have written in to Weird Central about it. Even school teachers and scientists have shared their stories.

In fact, in 1976, a group of scientists used their expertise in weather, physics, and chemistry to analyze what was going on. They found that there's a lot of seismic activity in the area that might be producing electrical charges.

daughter, Elizabeth Yuba. One day, when Johnny was chopping wood, he saw Elizabeth walking past and was distracted for a moment. He swung his ax—and missed the log he was aiming for. The ax hit his leg instead, and the cut was so serious, he died. Now, the hardworking woodcutter has a chance to play all day and night, and he seems to be enjoying himself. Nobody has ever had a scary story about the Toys "R" Us ghost. And whenever they catch the scent of flowers, they imagine that Johnny's about to give a present to Elizabeth on the site where he last saw her.

Attention, Shoppers . . . Ghost in Aisle 15C

Lots of people visit the Toys "R" Us on El Camino in **Sunnyvale, California**, but it's not just for the sales. Sometimes it's to check out the mysterious presence there—the famous Toys "R" Us ghost. The people who work there swear that something weird's going on in that store. When they open up the store in the morning, the floors they tidied up the night before are strewn with toys from the shelves. As they walk around, balls bounce off the shelves behind them and follow them down the aisles. Some people even claim they have seen teddy bears floating in the air in front of them! And on Aisle 15C, people catch the scent of freshly cut flowers, even though there are no flowers in the store. That's right—Toys "R" Us has a spectral smell!

They say that the person responsible for all these strange sights and smells was an orchard worker from the 1880s. At that time, Sunnyvale was covered with orchards, including the site where the toy store now stands. The worker's name was Johnny Johnson, and he had fallen in love with the farmer's

Today's Special at Walmart: Ghosts in the Toy Aisle

On the island of Galveston on the **Texas** coast, there's a Walmart with a haunted toy aisle. Every night, it seems, balls and boxes and toys are knocked off the shelves and found scattered in the aisle. The employees there have to tidy the place up every morning. Moving the toy section to another location doesn't make any difference.

It's not scary—but it is a mystery. Nobody's really sure what's going on. However, Galveston's history does provide some clues. The island has suffered many hurricanes over the years, including a very serious one in 1900. They say that many children who lived in an orphanage where the Walmart now stands were victims of that hurricane. Perhaps it's those children who now enjoy themselves in the darkened toy aisle.

A Noisy Night at the Talbott Tavern

Recently a colleague of ours at Weird Central took a trip to **Bardstown, Kentucky**, and stayed for a night at a beautiful eighteenth-century stagecoach inn called the Talbott Tavern. The innkeeper told our friend that she and her companion were the only two people staying in the inn that night, and added, "The ghosts will have someone to keep them company." Our friend shrugged off his comment as an attempt to scare them.

After the innkeeper left at about 7 PM, she heard all kinds of banging noises outside the door to her room, but when she went to investigate there was no one there. The minute she turned off the room lights, she heard the sound of a door slam loudly, a man sneeze, and then loud footsteps going down the hall. Then the door to the room banged a few times, as if someone grabbed the doorknob and tried to push the door open. She heard all kinds of noises throughout the rest of the inn: a bell chimed eleven times at 4 AM, horses' hooves clomped outside the window, three men talked and laughed till morning, and more. The next morning our friend said to the staff, "So, this place is haunted." They said that they've learned to live with the ghosts and that they're just playful and noisy, but never hurtful.

The Water Babies of Pyramid Lake

One of the best fishing spots in the United States is Pyramid Lake in northwestern **Nevada**. But if you go there and relax and cast your line, you might hear a strange noise coming from the murky depths. It might sound like a crying baby or a cat's mournful meowing. Take a word of advice before you dive into the cold water to rescue the poor, drowning creature that's calling for help. It might be a water baby! And if that sounds cute, think again.

According to legends of the Native American Paiute tribe, the water babies of Pyramid Lake aren't much bigger than babies, but they have the bodies of old men and the long hair of girls. To the Paiute, the water babies meant certain death. They were convinced that the little predators were responsible for many drownings and disappearances at Pyramid Lake. Paiute tribesmen who waded into the lake, following the call of the water babies, were never seen again.

Surprisingly, there's some physical evidence to support these Water Baby tales. Tiny footprints cover a rock in Owens Valley, a town on the border between California and Nevada.

Ghosts at Eastern State Penitentiary

What kind of house is haunted by the angriest, saddest ghosts? A "big house," of course. *The big house* is slang for a prison, and back when it was first built, there was no bigger "big house" than Eastern State Penitentiary in **Philadelphia, Pennsylvania**. There was no sadder place either. Prisoners were stuck in windowless rooms and never met anyone except guards and the occasional priest or minister. The idea was that criminals would have plenty of time to think about how bad they'd been—but this extended "time-out" caused many of them to go crazy. And, apparently, it kept them crazy even after they died.

This old prison closed in the 1970s, and it's now a museum—and the site of the scariest Halloween haunted house in the world, "Terror Behind the Walls." But the terror lurks behind the walls even when Halloween's over. In Cellblock 12, many people have heard the hollow and distant sound of laughter from empty cells. Shadowy apparitions lurk in the cells and the hallways. And people keep seeing darting shadows out of the corners of their eyes. One of these shadows lurks in the older cellblocks, unnoticed until you get too close to him, and he runs away. During a big restoration project, a locksmith named Gary Johnson was scared by this shadowy specter as he worked:

"I had this feeling that I was being watched," said Mr. Johnson, "There's nobody there. A couple of seconds later and I get the same feeling . . . I turn around . . . *shoooom* . . . this black shadow just leaped across the block!"

The worst thing about the ghosts at Eastern State is that they all seem to be angry. People who see them get a cold, dark feeling about their encounters. Not all ghostly meetings are like this though so take our advice: if you scare easily, don't go ghost hunting at Eastern State Penitentiary.

Check it out!
www.easternstate.org

65

Unrest in Cheesman Park

Cheesman Park is a pleasant and leafy public place in the city of **Denver, Colorado**, but it has a strange and creepy past that makes some people uneasy. From 1858 to 1890, the land that's now Cheesman Park was the city cemetery. After thirty-two years, the U.S. government said that the land didn't belong to the city. Officials then made a frightening announcement. The dead needed to be dug up and reburied somewhere else! Any bodies left unclaimed after three months would be disposed of!

Three months later, an undertaker named E. F. McGovern brought in teams of men to deal with the more than 5,000 unclaimed bodies. The men were told to dig up everyone and move them to Riverside Cemetery. It didn't take long for the workmen to get spooked. They swapped stories about an old woman who warned them to whisper a prayer over every body . . . or the dead would return. One workman named Jim Astor felt a ghost land on his shoulders. He was so frightened that he ran for his life. People in nearby homes saw confused spirits in their houses or knocking on their doors and windows in the night. Low moaning sounds drifted over the field of open graves—a sound that people still hear in Cheesman Park. These days, some people see misty figures and strange wandering shadows under the shade trees in the park. Is it overactive imaginations, or are these shadows the ghosts of people buried in the old City Cemetery, wondering where their bodies went? Who knows! We don't. But we get kind of scared thinking about it.

Strolling Through Baltimore After Death

As the oldest part of **Baltimore, Maryland,** Fell's Point is a fun place for tourists and city folk to go. In fact, it's so much fun to wander the streets there, at least two people continue to do it long after their deaths! We learned about them after a road trip in the Weirdmobile one evening. We decided to go on one of the area's famous night-time ghost walks. As we strolled past one of our favorite Weird places—a tiny one-grave cemetery on Shakespeare Street—our guide stopped us. "Did you know that four members of the Fell family lie buried there?" he asked. We did (we read a lot of books!). "And did you know that a ghost—maybe the ghost of one of them—walks down this street sometimes?" We didn't (apparently, we don't read enough!). "Well, he does. He starts at the top of the street, but by the time he gets halfway to the Bond Cemetery, he starts to fade away. He always vanishes before he reaches this point." We were impressed, but not as impressed as we were ten minutes later, when we rounded a quiet street a few blocks from the famous (and also haunted) Bertha's restaurant. A small private house down this street features another ghost. Our guide seemed anxious to keep clear of the front door. He seemed nervous and confided in us quietly, "I don't like that building much. If you stand too near the front door, you sometimes feel something shoving you from the front step of the porch. The ghost, whoever he is, doesn't like people too near his house." And with that, he moved us along quickly to an intersection with better light. We all felt a little better to be away from that place.

The next time you're in Baltimore, Maryland, stop by Bertha's restaurant for some great seafood and ghostly company.

A CREEPY CREATURE EXPEDITION

If you want to see exotic animals, all you have to do is go to the zoo or take a book out of the library. But, if you're looking for something a little more on the bizarre side, you may have to wait for a firsthand weird encounter. Maybe your parents' car will get a flat tire on a long stretch of abandoned road and you'll gaze out into the woods only to see something incredibly strange peering back at you. Or, perhaps you'll see something out of the corner of your eye during a hike. You may have trouble describing it later on, but the mere memory will make the hair on your arm stand straight up even weeks later. The strange class of creature we're talking about here doesn't show up in textbooks. In fact, they're almost never photographed and have, in many cases, remained hidden for centuries, seen only in glimpses. These creepy creatures never stick around long enough for scientists to study, although they do have a scientific name: cryptids, which is a word that means "hidden creatures." These creatures include serpents, devils, sea monsters, really hairy humanoids, and even a giant moth. You may not have spotted any of these cryptids in your hometown, but they're all over the U.S.!

Bigfoot

The most famous of all America's hidden creatures is Bigfoot. His name first appeared in print in a **California** newspaper in the 1950s, and it was meant as a joke. The reporters at the *Humboldt Times* didn't believe tales of a tall, hairy ape-man in the woods because the only evidence left behind was a set of huge footprints. So the nickname Bigfoot seemed like a good one. Most people who take Bigfoot seriously call him by its Native American name: Sasquatch. In Florida, they call him the Skunk Ape. He's also called BHM (which is short for Big Hairy Man), and in other countries, they call similar creatures Yeti, Yeren, and Yowie.

Many of the names they give Bigfoot are pretty silly, but when people have Bigfoot encounters in the woods, they don't laugh about it. For one thing, this is a very large animal—seven or eight feet tall, or even taller, people say. He skulks around in the trees in remote areas, mostly hidden from sight, which is enough to creep anybody out. And he sometimes gives off a horrible smell, which may be a defensive feature like skunk spray. And Bigfoot can be aggressive. He's been known to throw rocks, smash though thick branches, and even uproot trees. Sasquatch doesn't usually attack people, but he makes a lot of noise trying to scare them away.

In short, Bigfoot just wants to be left alone. He lives in remote places and does his best to keep people away. So no matter what you call him, this two-legged titan looks like no other animal. Is it an ape? Is it almost human? Is it an ancient species like the extra-tall ape-man gigantopithecus, which we had assumed was extinct? We don't know. The answers, like Sasquatch himself, remain hidden. Bigfoot has been sighted in **Washington, California, Florida, Texas, Maryland, New Jersey** . . . pretty much anywhere there are secluded woody areas near running water.

Most Bigfoot tracks have five toes, but three-toed tracks have been found in Maryland. Perhaps there's more than one species of Bigfoot!

The most famous Bigfoot evidence was a home movie shot in 1967 by Roger Patterson. It was shot on a trail in remote **Northern California.** Some people think it shows a human in an ape suit. But zoologists who look at the film say that the arms are much too long for a human and swing in an apelike way. Besides . . . you can't see a zipper anywhere!

Cryptids from the Deep

What's the first name that pops into your head when people talk about giant serpents that live in lakes? We're betting it's Nessie, the Loch Ness Monster. But the U.S. has its own giant water creatures. Some live in lakes and some in salty seawater. According to the people who have seen them, most seem to have large snakelike bodies with horselike heads—just like the creature in the movie *The Water Horse: Legend of the Deep*. Some people think that there's an entire species of large water creatures—maybe some kind of dinosaur that isn't extinct. Others think that these stories are exaggerated, and whatever people see in the water is probably an eel or large fish. We don't know what the real story is—but we've been collecting reports from across the States. Here are a few of them.

The Champ

The first European to clap eyes on **Lake Champlain in New York/Vermont** was Samuel de Champlain, so he got to name the lake. This was back in 1609, but even back then he noticed something weird about the place: it had a twenty-foot-long snakelike creature in it. People have been spotting this creature ever since and have given it an affectionate name: Champ.

Tahoe Tessie

Lake Tahoe in **northern California** is a deep, dark lake with several odd legends around it. One talks of a lake monster they call Tessie. Another mentions hundreds of dead humans bobbing around deep beneath the surface—people who have drowned but are kept from turning into skeletons by the near-freezing water. Although experts say this never happened, some people insist that the famous underwater explorer Jacques Cousteau took a mini submarine and camera down into the depths of Lake Tahoe and came back saying, "The world is not ready to see what's down there." And the film was never shown to anybody. So what did he see down there? A strange lake creature that was too hideous for the public to see? An underwater graveyard? Or something even more mysterious? It's possible the world will never know.

Chessie of Chesapeake Bay

Chessie isn't a lake monster like her rhyming relatives Nessie, Bessie, and Tessie. She doesn't live in freshwater at all, but in **Maryland's** salty **Chesapeake Bay**. So she's a sea serpent that's probably part of a whole family: giant serpents with horselike heads have been seen in the Chesapeake since the 1800s, sometimes in groups of four or more. So we're convinced that there's something out of the ordinary swimming around the bay. But what can it be?

If you want to know the answer to a tough question like that, it helps to ask an expert. Fortunately, one of Chessie's eyewitnesses was trained in wildlife management, so he knew what to look for. Robert Frew and his wife, Karen, saw and videotaped something that might have been Chessie in 1982, and Mr. Frew noticed a lot of details. The creature moved from side to side like a snake, and it swam in water that was only five feet deep. Other zoologists looked at Mr. Frew's videotape, and they concluded it was a brownish eel-like creature as round as a telephone pole, with humps on its back.

South Bay Bessie

Lake Erie is a good name for parts of the Great Lake that run across the north of Ohio and touch bits of western Pennsylvania and New York State. It just needs an extra "e"—because at night, it can be one eerie place, especially if you run into a forty-foot-long gray snake. That's what a reporter for the **Sandusky, Ohio**, newspaper the *Daily Register* thought back in 1898, when he reported on the creature we now call South Bay Bessie.

"For a number of years, vague stories about huge serpents have come with each recurring season," he wrote. "Now, at last, the existence of these fierce monsters is verified."

He went on to report sightings of "a fierce, ugly, coiling thing, call it a snake or what you will," which moves on land and water, and was at least one foot thick. The creature became a bit of a joke after this, however, and many later articles on the subject came out on April 1 to fool the public. One year, some hoaxers pretended to have caught it, only to have the creature identified as an Indian python. So is Bessie a big fish? A foreign snake? Or a bona fide lake monster? We don't know . . . what do you think?

The Jersey Devil

For nearly 300 years, **New Jersey** residents have been swapping stories of a strange creature that lives in the spookiest place in the state—the thick forest called the Pine Barrens. These stories tell of a creature with a dog or horse's head, a kangaroo's body, and batlike wings. Some say it has antlers, human legs, and a forked tail. In short, we're talking about a whole zoo rolled into one dragonlike creature. They call him the Jersey Devil.

Like superheroes in comic books, creatures in dark woods must have gotten their strange appearance from somewhere. That's why the most popular story about the Jersey Devil is the story of his origin. It goes something like this: Many years ago, an unhappy woman named Mother Leeds discovered she was expecting a baby. She already had twelve children, and her husband didn't work much or help around the house. She got so angry, she said, "Let this one be a devil!" and stomped about in a temper. When she finally delivered her baby, he was a normal little boy, but almost immediately, he started to change. His face began to grow long and strange looking. Bumps formed on his back that sprouted into wings. His feet changed into something inhuman. And he went on a wild rampage. Some say he killed his brothers and sisters. Others say he hurt his mother. But they all say he escaped up the chimney and has been rampaging through the Pine Barrens ever since.

Most people treat the Jersey Devil as a strange old legend, like Paul Bunyan (with added bat wings). But don't let that fool you. People don't spot Paul Bunyan

The Jersey Devil captured and stuffed?

The Pine Barrens, where the Jersey Devil has been spotted.

THE NEW JERSEY "WHAT-IS-IT," AS NELSON EVANS
SAYS HE SAW IT ON HIS SHED ROOF AT 2 A. M.

*Philadelphia
Evening Bulletin*

in the woods of south Jersey, but we do hear from people who have seen the Jersey Devil—or something they think is the Jersey Devil. So we treat him like the real thing—a hidden creature with some great stories stuck to him—and we wait for the sightings to come rolling in.

We're talking about a whole zoo rolled into one dragonlike creature!

The Mothman Cometh!

Everybody knows that moths are attracted to light. Leave your curtains open on a summer night and look at how many of the little critters bop their heads against the glass. But did you know that there's a creature from West Virginia that actually provides the light? Two red lights, to be exact . . . where his eyes belong. It also has huge wings and is shaped like a man. And that's why they call it the Mothman. It's become such a local celebrity that **Point Pleasant, West Virginia** (where it was first spotted), throws a Mothman Festival (check it out at www.mothmanfestival.com) in its honor every year on the third weekend in September. There's even a big Mothman statue in Gunn Park in the town.

So where did Mothman come from, and what does it want? Nobody knows. It was first spotted in 1966, late one night, by two couples. Its body was man shaped, but it had huge wings that went far above its head, wrapped around its sides, and dragged on the ground behind it. Its eyes were the first things they noticed— they were red and glowing.

For a year afterward, lots of people saw it, and they were scared. One man thought he saw the Mothman and shot at it—only to find that he'd killed a snowy owl instead. Other people started saying it might be an alien creature, or the result of a Native American curse. When a local bridge collapsed, people were so hysterical about the Mothman that they tried to blame it on the creature. But one of the first people to see Mothman, Linda Scarberry, got to see it many times, and realized it wasn't as scary as it seemed at first sight. Linda spoke to us at Weird Central. She told us what she saw that night out by the Point Pleasant powerhouse, and how she kept seeing it afterward.

"We saw it dozens of times. It was at our apartment . . . sitting up there on the roof. At first, I was really afraid of it, but it had so many chances to hurt us, and it didn't seem like it wanted to. It acted like it was trying to communicate with us through its eyes."

It's been more than forty years now since Mothman first appeared, and we still don't know much about it. Some people think that a lot of Mothman sightings

You may not run into Mothman if you visit Point Pleasant, but you can always visit his statue! Way creepy!

may be cases of mistaken identity. There's a huge bird called the sandhill crane that has huge wings like those on the Mothman. Maybe that crane accounts for some of the sightings. But other sightings aren't so easy to dismiss. What do you think? Is it a bird? Is it a plane? Or is it some strange creature from another world? Your guess is as good as ours —maybe even better!

Many people blamed Mothman for the 1967 collapse of the Silver Bridge, in which forty-six people died.

Lizard Man

The story of the Lizard Man of Scape Ore Swamp sounds like something you tell around a campfire to scare people. But it's been reported in newspapers and on CNN. A teenager in **Lee County, South Carolina**, was driving home late one night, when his tire blew out. As he finished fixing the flat, he heard a thumping noise coming up behind him. He turned and saw something incredible. Seven feet tall. Scaly. Green. Running toward him on two legs. It looked like a man wrapped in lizard skin with glowing red eyes!

The teenager, Christopher Davis, made a run for the driver's seat and started to drive away when the creature reached the door. Thank goodness the door was locked. As the creature grabbed the door handle, Christopher saw it had only three fingers, with long black fingernails and rough dark skin. He accelerated away, but the creature leaped onto the car roof and clawed at the windows. Christopher swerved, turned, skidded, and finally managed to shake off the creature.

When he reported this incident to the police, officials were skeptical. They thought it more likely that the damage was caused by careless driving and that the teen was attempting to keep out of trouble by blaming it on a monster attack. But they changed their minds when other people began reporting strange claw marks on their cars—and a large creature that even chewed on their cars. Two weeks later, the sheriff's department investigated strange three-toed footprints down at the swamp, more than fourteen inches long. All this happened in the summer of 1988, and fortunately for the good folks of Lee County, sightings tailed off that same year. Every so often, people report seeing a creature in the swamp, but whoever or whatever the Lizard Man might be, he seems to be keeping his distance from humanity right now. Next time you're in the swamps of South Carolina, pray that he doesn't change his mind.

A Goatman bridge crossing White Rock Lake in Texas.

Goatman

Of all the strange, legendary creatures in the United States, the Goatman of **Maryland** is the one that sounds like a really old legend. He's half man, half goat, just like the satyrs of ancient Greek legends. His legs are covered with thick fur and end up in hooves instead of feet, but from the waist up he looks almost human. His head, of course, has horns sprouting from it, which makes him look devilish and scary.

His story goes back to the 1950s, when some scientists were hard at work in the Beltsville Agricultural Research Center in Prince George's County, just outside of Washington D.C. They were performing strange Frankenstein-style experiments with animals, trying to make them more profitable for farmers. One of their experiments went horribly wrong. Instead of producing a goat that could give more milk, they produced a strange hybrid goat creature that looked part human. This mutant goat used his human intelligence to escape, and once out in the open, he hid in the woods and avoided capture.

Goatman stories tend to center around Bowie, especially Lottsford Road and Governor's Bridge Road. There's an iron bridge across the Patuxent that is sometimes called the Goatman Bridge. Since the earliest reports in 1957, the Bowie area has had the most Goatman sightings and stories—though stories of half-goat, half-human creatures have more recently come in from **Texas, Indiana**, and half a dozen other states. This is one tragic figure that gets around!

Thunderbirds

Giant flying creatures have been the stuff of legend for hundreds of years. In Europe, people used to swap stories about birds so large they could carry off sheep, small cows, and even humans. Here in America, various Native American tribes have legends of enormous winged monsters, like the Illini tribe's tales of the Piasa Bird (that's pronounced *pie-a-saw*) and the Ojibwa stories of the Thunderbird.

These stories could have started because people saw fossils of enormous flying dinosaurs and assumed that some living examples were still kicking around somewhere. Perhaps they saw some huge bald eagle or condor and thought it was even bigger than it really is. Or maybe there's something more to these stories. In 1868 in **Tippah County, Missouri**, an eight-year-old boy was carried off by what was described as an eagle. The teacher who saw this happen states that he could only hear the boy's screaming as he vanished into the sky. The teacher raised the alarm in town, and the noise must have frightened the bird—it dropped the boy, dead. Now, considering even the most powerful eagle could only lift a rabbit, what do you suppose carried away that boy?

In 1948, a former army colonel in **Alton, Illinois**, saw a gigantic bird in the sky. "It was definitely a bird and not a glider or a jet plane. I figured it could only be a bird of tremendous size," he said. A few days later, a St. Louis woman saw the bird from her apartment window as it swerved to avoid crashing into a plane. The bird was reported for the last time about a month after it first appeared.

Thirty years later in Lawndale, Illinois, reports came in of two huge birds swooping down from the sky and attacking three boys who were playing in the backyard of Ruth and Jake Lowe. One of the birds grabbed the shirt of ten-year-old Marlon Lowe. Marlon's mother ran outside to see the bird lift the boy three feet from the ground and then carry him up about thirty-five feet. She screamed and the bird released the child, who was not seriously injured. She described the birds as black with

bands of white around their necks. They had long, curved beaks and wingspans of at least ten feet.

These are puzzling tales with no easy answers. Are these mysterious flying creatures real? If not, then what have so many people been witnessing over the years? One thing is for certain: the sightings have continued. So next time you're standing in a field and a dark shadow fills the sky, ask yourself: was that just a cloud passing in front of the sun . . . or was it something else?

That Can't Be Real!

Most of the bizarre beasts we've looked at so far don't leave much solid evidence behind them. But there's another kind of strange creature. These beasts appear in sideshows or museums around the country, stuffed and mounted in glass display cases for people to look at. They look like real animals. People claim they are real. But they seem so strange that they just have to be clever fakes. Take a look at the pictures in this section and see if you think they're real or fake.

Exhibit #2: The Sea Devil

For more than 500 years, sailors have entertained us landlubbers with tales of flying devils from the sea. Sometimes, they even produced evidence of the attacks—dried-out creatures with wings, sharp teeth, and sunken eyes. Somewhere along the line, these creatures got the name Jenny Haniver, and their carcasses would travel across the United States with carnivals and sideshows. You can still find them in museums sometimes (Baltimore's now-closed American Dime Museum once had two).

Exhibit #1: The Jackalope

Here's a question for you: what one thing do the Wichita Art Museum, the Wyoming town of Douglas, and the University of Kansas Natural History Museum have in common? Well, it looks like a jackrabbit, it hops like a jackrabbit, and it has horns like an antelope. That's right . . . it's a jackalope. These museums contain stuffed examples of the creature. And the town of Douglas claims to be its hometown.

Exhibit #4: Furry Fish

Since Europeans first settled in America, tales of one strange-looking fish have spread through Montana, Wyoming, and Colorado. The fish in question is a trout that survives the freezing waters by growing a thick layer of fur in wintertime. You can see one of these furry trouts at the Creation Museum and Taxidermy Hall of Fame in **Southern Pines, North Carolina.**

Exhibit #3: Mermaids

People have been telling stories about mermaids for thousands of years, but it's only recently—in the past 200 years—that people have produced any evidence. Or is it fake evidence? In the 1820s, an American sea captain named Samuel Barrett Eades exhibited a mermaid he had bought from an exotic location. This was not the attractive half-woman that most people think of when they think of mermaids. The top part was a furry, ugly monkey-faced creature; the bottom half was a fish tail.

Captain Eades didn't make much money by exhibiting his mermaid, but the next man who owned it made a fortune. He was the famous showman P. T. Barnum, and when he put his FeeJee Mermaid into a sideshow tent, people swarmed to see it. You can still see examples of these sorts of mermaids at various places around the States. There's one in Delaware's most weirdly named museum—the Zwaanendael Museum in Lewes—and another at Harvard's Peabody Museum of Archaeology and Ethnology.

Real or Fake?

Exhibit #1: The Jackalope

Even though a man from Douglas produced the first example of the horned jackrabbit in 1939, it's highly unlikely that jackalopes exist in the wild. The examples we've seen are what carnival operators call gaffs—creative fakes put together by clever artists. Instead of doing what taxidermists usually do—simply prepare dead animals for display—they use authentic animal parts from several different animals and make a Frankenstein's monster out of them.

Exhibit #2: The Sea Devil

Well, they're real animals. But they're also fakes. The sailors took dead flat fish, usually skates or rays, and carved them up into strange creations. Then they let them dry out in the sun, varnished them, and mounted them. When the sailors got to shore, they'd tell wild stories and sell their handiwork to whoever offered the most money.

Exhibit #3: Mermaids

Way back before P. T. Barnum displayed his FeeJee Mermaid, scientists had figured out the creature was a hoax made from a stuffed ape carefully sewn to the tail of a large salmon. But people still visited the exhibit back then, just as they still do today.

Exhibit #4: Furry Fish

Fish don't grow fur, even in cold climates. The story may have started as a joke or it may have been a genuine misunderstanding—there is a fungus that grows on some sick fish that looks like hair—but every example that's stuffed and mounted in a museum is a fake.

A GUIDED TOUR OF THE UNKNOWN

Chapter 7

"I offer the data. Suit yourself."

These words were written by Charles Fort (1874–1932), and this chapter is full of the type of data that he specialized in: floating lights and UFOs, tales about people with unbelievable powers, and incidents of curious objects falling from the sky.

A true believer in uncertainty and a crank with a wicked sense of humor, Charles Fort loved poking fun at scientists by gathering together stories that scientists couldn't explain. He called his findings "weird observations," and he researched and recorded so many that the study of strange phenomena is often called *Forteana*. Of course, Charles Fort is one of our *Weird* heroes, and we like to think that we're doing our bit to carry on his work. So, in the spirit of Charles Fort, we've gathered together some Fortean goodies that you can visit!

Is this stuff for real? Or is it all pure invention, concocted by people with overactive imaginations? Or does the truth lie somewhere in between, in a region that Fort liked to call, "the borderland between fact and fantasy?" Read on and decide for yourself.

The Marfa Lights

Charles Fort called them "auroras." Modern paranormal investigators call them by a variety of names: ghost lights, spooklights, mystery lights, earthlights, fireballs, and anomalous luminous phenomena. In **Presidio County, Texas**, they've inherited the name of the closest town, Marfa.

The Marfa lights are mysterious, floating balls of light that are spotted at night about nine miles east of Marfa. On any night and in any kind of weather, they might flare up for a crowd of curious onlookers. Most often, the orbs are white, yellow, or orange, but occasionally, red, blue, or green lights have been reported. Their behavior is equally unpredictable. They might hover above the ground, glide across the sky, or bounce around haphazardly in random directions. As you're watching, one light might split into two or two lights might merge into one and then disappear, only to reappear a moment later. Mystifying, captivating, and strangely beautiful, the playful dance of the Marfa lights has been attracting attention for more than a hundred years.

A Native American legend connects the lights to the spirit of an Apache chief named Chinati. Skeptics often insist that the lights are just reflections of car headlights from the road across the way. Yet, this theory doesn't explain the variety of colors or the weird movement of the lights. Many scientists assume that the Marfa lights are associated with some kind of electrical discharge, but research on the subject has been inconclusive.

The mystery behind the ghost lights of Marfa has made the town a popular tourist attraction. Thrilled by the attention, Presidio County has responded by building an official Marfa Lights viewing area.

Check it out!
www.marfacc.com

Great Green Balls of Fire!

Between 1948 and 1951, strange green fireballs in the skies above **New Mexico** had government officials baffled. Military officials and scientists converged on **Los Alamos** and decided that the lights were not meteorites and were therefore of an unknown origin. Some believed that they were test firings of some sort of extraterrestrial weaponry. No one ever figured out what these lights were.

UFO Capitals of the World

It sounds like a simple question to answer: what's the UFO capital of the world? However, like most questions that seem simple at first, you get a lot of different answers depending on whom you ask. Surprisingly, there are almost as many towns claiming this prize as there are pizzerias advertising theirs as "the world's best pizza." So, why not visit all these places that claim to have been visited by aliens!

Roswell, New Mexico

July 1947 is a very important month in the world of ufology. According to UFO enthusiasts, that's when a flying saucer crashed near **Roswell, New Mexico**. They insist that what followed was a massive cover-up by the U.S. government. The legend goes like this: a spaceship and the bodies of the aliens aboard were removed from the area and relocated to a secret place where they could be studied. Of course, the official story is more believable—and quite a bit less interesting. The Roswell Army Air Field (RAAF) reported that the unidentified flying object recovered near Roswell was actually a weather balloon.

More than sixty years have passed, but the events of July 1947 remain mysterious and controversial. And Roswell, New Mexico, now seems to have embraced "the Roswell incident." Stores around town proudly display fake crashed saucers and statues of little green men. Also, Roswell offers many alien-themed tourist attractions, like the Cover-up Café and the International UFO Museum. There are even rumors that a UFO theme park is in the works. These days, if aliens actually landed in Roswell, they would probably be mobbed by tourists seeking autographs.

Be sure to visit the International UFO Museum, where you can witness a grisly "reenactment" of an alien autopsy. Check it out at www.roswellufomuseum.com!

These images of the wreckage were taken before the cover-up.

Rachel, Nevada

If you believe the Roswell legend, then where do you think the government keeps the evidence? Many believe that the hiding place is a top-secret military base in Nevada called Area 51.

You can drive to Area 51 by taking the Extraterrestrial Highway. (We're not kidding! The State of Nevada renamed the highway in 1996.) After a long, flat stretch of desert, you'll drive into the town of Rachel. The welcome sign says it all:

Population—Humans 98, Aliens ?

Rachel, Nevada, is a tiny town with a good sense of humor and a fascination for all things extraterrestrial. You'll find the Area 51 Gift Shop and a cozy hotel/restaurant called the Little A'Le'Inn ("A-li-en"—get it?). (Check it out at www.littlealeinn.com!) The place is easy to spot because, out front, there's a tow truck hoisting a little flying saucer. A warning: if you decide to explore Area 51, remember that it's restricted. You might get chased away by mysterious government agents in dark suits, known as the Men in Black.

Take me to your gift shops.

Dundee, Wisconsin

Or **Elmwood, Wisconsin** . . . or **Belleville, Wisconsin** . . . Based on the number of UFO sightings in Wisconsin, we could have picked any of these towns. But **Dundee** is more than just a UFO hot spot. It's the home of the annual UFO Daze Festival.

Festivalgoers come from all over to share UFO stories and scan the night skies, searching for alien spaceships. Many wear tinfoil hats to prevent aliens from reading their minds. Better to look silly than get your mind probed by an extraterrestrial, don't you think? Dundee also has a spokesperson for extraterrestrial matters. His name is Robert Kuehn, but most people know him as UFO Bob. The leader behind UFO Daze, and the host of a radio show about aliens, UFO Bob says that he has been abducted more than once. That would have been enough to turn most people against E.T.s, but, for UFO Bob, these experiences have given him a rare understanding of space aliens, whom he views as friends. "They want recognition," he announced at a recent UFO Daze fest. "So take your flashlights outside tonight and shine them around in the sky."

Triangles, Vortexes & Interdimensional Gateways

Ever wish that the tree or rock in your backyard could whisk you away to another time, place, or even planet? As weird as this may sound, these kinds of places may really exist! Triangles and vortexes. Holes in the fabric of space and time. These twilight zones are called by many names and are considered hot spots for all kinds of paranormal phenomenas. They are regions where weirdness rules, where Bigfoot frolics with man-sized birds and space aliens, and human beings vanish.

So, step lively, and watch out for interdimensional holes. We're going on a cross-country vortex vacation!

The Bridgewater Triangle

Maybe you've heard of the Bermuda Triangle, a mysterious region in the Atlantic Ocean that's like a paranormal roach trap for ships and planes. (They go in but never come out!) Did you know that there's another strange triangle in **Massachusetts** called "The Bridgewater Triangle"? **Abington, Freetown,** and **Rehoboth** are the points of the triangle. If you take a map of the state and draw lines connecting these towns, then you'll have outlined one of the weirdest areas in Weird America. And if you look smack in the middle of the triangle, you'll see the creepy centerpiece of the Bridgewater Triangle, a 17,000-acre marsh called Hockomock Swamp. The name Hockomock comes from Native Americans who were both impressed and frightened by the spooky wetland. Roughly translated from their language, the word means "place of spirits."

From the ghost stories we've heard, spirits seem very much at home in the Bridgewater Triangle. Many people have spotted Native American phantom warriors dressed in battle garb. Other witnesses have reported beautiful displays of ghost light activity: mysterious orbs hovering above the ground, changing colors from red to blue to orange, and then suddenly disappearing. But the weirdness of the Bridgewater Triangle extends far past sightings of ghosts and fireballs.

In 1979, a newsman was driving inside the Bridgewater Triangle when he saw flying above him a UFO shaped like a giant baseball home plate. Eight years earlier, policeman Thomas Downy was patrolling near a spot called Bird Hill when he saw something unexpected: a giant bird, more than six feet tall with an eight- to twelve-foot wingspan! In paranormal circles, these

The Redheaded Hitcher of Route 44

Rehoboth, Massachusetts, is one of the corners of the Bridgewater Triangle, so if your family is traveling on Route 44 between Seekonk and Rehoboth, you may not want to pick up hitchhikers. This is particularly true if the hitcher happens to have messy red hair and a curly, bushy beard, and is wearing a flannel shirt and an old pair of blue jeans. From the description, this may sound more like a lumberjack than an evil spirit. But looks can be deceiving.

There are quite a few local legends about ghost hitchhikers, but there's something unusually unsettling about the Redheaded Hitcher of Route 44. He's been spotted thumbing a ride on this five-mile stretch of highway many times since 1969, and his exploits are documented in the 1994 book *The New England Ghost Files*, written by Charles Robinson. One witness was in his car when he noticed the hitcher's grinning face pressed up against the passenger window. Needless to say, the driver was shocked, especially since, at that moment, the car was speeding along at about fifty miles an hour. Shaken up, the man pulled to the side of the road and glanced over to find that the maniacal face was gone. The prankster spirit struck again on February 25, 1981. He materialized in the middle of the road, frightening a woman who was traveling on Route 44. She slammed on her brakes, skidded, and swerved. Out of control, her car barreled into the figure. Distraught, she was convinced that she'd struck and killed a man, but when she stepped out to check, she couldn't find his body. Standing on the lonely highway, she was confronted by menacing laughter, coming from the dark woods beside her.

For his next victims, the redheaded hitcher picked an unfortunate husband and wife. Their station wagon broke down on Route 44, and the man went in search of help, leaving his wife behind. Trudging up the empty road, the husband spotted a redheaded stranger sitting on the shoulder of the highway. Approaching the fellow, he asked where he could find a telephone. The scraggly haired ghost said nothing, but a devilish smile formed on his face. When the husband repeated his question, the ghoul began cackling. "The laughing kept switching locations," the witness told Mr. Robinson. "First I heard it in front of me, then behind me, then to the left of me. It was bizarre. I began to run along the highway back toward the car, and, as I did, the laughing followed me for a good two or three hundred feet. It scared the heck out of me. And then suddenly it stopped." The husband fled back to his wife and learned that she had also had a terrifying experience. While she was waiting in the car, she had heard the deep shrieking laughter of the redheaded ghost . . . coming from the car radio!

pterodactyl-like creatures are called Thunderbirds (see page 78). And, true to its name, Bird Hill is famous for Thunderbird sightings. Some have even insisted that the flying creature they saw wasn't a bird at all but a man with wings! Others have seen enormous manlike apes (Bigfoot?) and gigantic, ferocious dogs (werewolves?). Where are all of these impossible creatures coming from? We can't say for sure. And until one of us steps through the interdimensional gateway at the heart of the Bridgewater Triangle, we'll probably never know.

The Bennington Triangle

Another mysterious portal to the unknown in New England is the Bennington Triangle, near **Glastenbury Mountain, Vermont**, not far from the town of Bennington. Like the Bridgewater Triangle, Glastenbury Mountain was said to be cursed by Native Americans. And early settlers of the region traded stories about ghosts, oversized animals, and floating balls of light.

But these tales of strange sightings were eclipsed in the 1940s and 1950s by a rash of unexplained disappearances. A seventy-four-year-old guide named Middie Rivers vanished on November 12, 1945, while he was leading a team of hunters down the mountain. An expert outdoorsman who grew up in the area, Mr. Rivers wandered ahead of the group and was never seen again. And then there was Jim Tedford, who got on a bus to Bennington but somehow never got off. When the bus driver arrived at the stop, the man was nowhere to be found.

In a span of five years, six people vanished in Glastenbury Mountain. Eventually, one body was recovered. Seven months after Freida Langer vanished, her corpse was found lying in the grass near Somerset Reservoir, right out in the open. How could hundreds of people in the search team have missed her? It's almost as if her body had reappeared as suddenly as it had vanished!

Red Rock Vortexes

Instead of scaring people away, the vortexes in **Sedona, Arizona**, have become a tourist attraction. Vortex guides are available to lead tours through the awesome red rock landscape. Some visitors believe that the vortexes found here are doorways to another dimension, but these folks haven't come to Sedona hoping to fall through a hole in space-time. They came to feel the energy!

Spiritualists insist that scattered about the spires and mesas in Sedona are energy power points. In these spots, trees grow in swirling spires, and sensitive humans feel a sudden pulse or a whoosh. Afterward, they feel calm and energized, often comparing the experience to "having their batteries recharged." Ghost lights are common in the area, and UFO sightings are frequent as well. In fact, there's a strange rumor among ufologists that a giant spaceship is hidden inside Bell Rock in Sedona. But wait! The rumor gets even weirder. We've heard that the vortex energy fields are coming from equipment left behind by space aliens!

The World's Slowest Racetrack

No place in the United States seems as otherworldly as **California's Death Valley**. Wandering through the surreal landscape, it's easy to imagine that you've materialized in a science-fiction film about Mars. The mysterious moving dolomite rocks of Racetrack Playa would perfectly suit the movie inside your head. Leaving a long trail behind them, these stones always seem still, but somehow, slowly but surely, over the course of years, they continue on their way. They almost seem . . . alive!

They're not, of course, but then what's making them move? The floor of the valley, a vast stretch of dried, cracked mud, is perfectly flat. According to the laws of gravity, these boulders should stay put. Could it be the wind? Not likely. The trails behind these rocks show zigzagging patterns, with different rocks meandering to and fro in random directions. Wind would certainly produce a more uniform path. And how did these rocks travel so far from the mountains they broke away from? These unanswerable questions, along with the unearthly beauty of Death Valley, make Racetrack Playa one of the must-see destinations in Weird America.

Gravity Hills

Gravity Hills. Magnetic Hills. Ghost Hills. Mystery Hills. Haunted Hills. Antigravity Hills. They're scattered around the world and are called by many names. But every gravity hill follows the same topsy-turvy logic. If you park on a gravity hill and you put your car into neutral, you'll find yourself rolling uphill instead of downhill. And if that sounds like magic to you, you're not alone, because these upside-down gravity spots are also known as Magic Hills.

Skeptics dismiss the phenomena as an optical illusion. They insist that the road looks like it's sloping downward, but it's actually sloping upward. Or vice versa. Supernaturalists tend to think that gravity hills are haunted and that spirits are nudging your car against gravity's pull. To prove these theories, ghost hunters sometimes sprinkle baby powder on their cars, hoping to capture phantom handprints. Some mystics insist that gravity hills are mysterious electromagnetic oddities where the laws of physics break down.

Whether you're a skeptic, a supernaturalist, a mystic, or just curious like the rest of us, you'll certainly agree that gravity hills are fun to experience. But a word of warning: riding backward up a hill is not safe, especially if other cars are around. We learned this lesson the hard way. Researching a gravity hill in **Bergen County, New Jersey**, we got in a little fender bender . . . with a police car! After the accident, the patrolman stepped out of his vehicle. Shaking his head, he began writing out a ticket. He didn't say a word. He didn't have to. He was standing beside a sign that read "Trying Out Gravity Road Is Not Permitted." Oops.

Going up???

Booger Hill

Just north of **Cumming, Georgia**, on Bettis Tribble Gap Road, is a gravity hill with a sad legend attached to it. According to the tale, on that spot a long time ago, a group of children died in an accident. They were all piled in a vehicle and the driver swerved to avoid a stalled car, and . . . crash! Ever since then, when the ghost kids spot a car stopped on the street, they think that it has stalled, so they try to push it uphill, out of the way of oncoming vehicles.

A writer named Michael Wehunt tested out Booger Hill and described the experience in *Flagpole* magazine. He applied baby powder to the car and after taking a few rides up the hill, he stepped out to look for evidence. On the rear hood and bumper, he found "hints of fingerprints" in the powder. He also noticed a letter "J" and other marks that looked like thin strands—like the streaks that would be left behind by a little girl's hair.

Spook Hill

Lake Wales, Florida, doesn't discourage visitors from taking a test drive on Spook Hill. Instead, they put up signs to advertise the phenomena. As a result, Lake Wales has become a Weird tourist attraction. On weekends, lines of cars show up and drivers patiently wait their turn, eager for a gravity-defying thrill ride.

In Lake Wales, many strange stories are told to help explain the weird antigravity effect. Some residents insist that a gigantic magnetic meteorite is buried somewhere inside the hill. Others mention Native American legends, saying that the hill is haunted by a vengeful alligator spirit or perhaps the ghost of a local warrior chief trying to protect his land. No theory is too strange for the townspeople of Lake Wales. They seem to have completely embraced Spook Hill, along with the spookiness that comes with it. In fact, when it came time to choose a mascot for Spook Hill Elementary School, the principal made the perfect choice: Casper the Friendly Ghost.

Mystery Spot

Mystery Spot is a magical place where the rules of gravity don't apply and the words "up" and "down" are meaningless concepts. It's a little shack on a hill in **Santa Cruz, California**, and inside it, odd forces are at play. Pool balls roll uphill. Chairs balance unexpectedly on two legs. People seem to grow and shrink as they shuffle about. Tilted and strange, the place makes you dizzy. You can even walk on the walls!

Is this just a funhouse, cleverly designed to be as confusing as possible? Or is it built upon some kind of electromagnetic hot spot? The explanation provided on the Mystery Spot's Web site (www.mysteryspot.com) involves some kind of "guidance system" for UFOs. This extraterrestrial technology is reportedly buried underneath the land and it bends the laws of gravity. And as an added bonus . . . while you're visiting the Mystery Spot, there are numerous gravity hills to check out in California.

There are Mystery Spots all across Weird America, including Cave City, Kentucky; Gold Hill, Oregon; Rapid City, South Dakota; Blowing Rock, North Carolina; and the one pictured above in St. Ignace, Michigan.

ROADS & BRIDGES BEST NOT TRAVELED

It's late, you're sitting in the car on the way home, and the person behind the wheel has taken a different route than usual. You're in unfamiliar territory. The car turns a corner and suddenly you begin to feel uneasy. Your heart starts pounding faster and you realize that you're trembling. The night seems darker and scarier than any you can remember. You ask yourself, "What is it about this road?"

All across the country there are infamous roads and bridges that drivers go out of their way to avoid. Some have unsettling names like Mount Misery Road or Green Hand Bridge. Some are associated with legends, weird tales about wandering spirits or prowling creatures. And some are just plain creepy—deserted and sinister. Are these spooky roads and bridges mystical hot spots? Are they evil? Haunted? Or is the danger all in our minds? We can't say for sure, but we'll wager that even a die-hard skeptic wouldn't be too thrilled to take a late-night ride on Shades of Death Road. Weird travelers don't avoid these roads and bridges—we seek them out! You're welcome to climb in the Weirdmobile and come along for a hair-raising, spine-tingling, goose-bumpy ride.

Shades of Death Road

No one knows exactly what they were they thinking when they named Shades of Death Road, but as far back as people can remember, this crooked lane in **Warren County, New Jersey**, has been associated with death and destruction. There are old yarns about man-eating wildcats, killer bandits, and fatal diseases. More recent tales come from police files. In one horrific case, a woman murdered her husband and buried his head and torso on opposite sides of Shades of Death Road. With a gruesome name and a gruesome history, it's not surprising that townspeople insist that this desolate and gloomy street is haunted.

Indian Curse Road

Officially it's called Route 55, but there's a stretch of highway between **Mantua and Franklin Township, New Jersey**, that's known to frightened locals as Indian Curse Road.

This disturbing nickname surfaced in 1983 when the section of highway was being built. Accidents plagued the project from the beginning. One worker was flattened by a steamroller, while another was overtaken by powerful winds and fell from an overpass. A van, which was carrying five employees from the Department of Transportation, caught fire and blew up. Machines broke constantly, and a terrified man working on the job complained that his feet had mysteriously turned black. Sachem Wayandaga, the chief of the Delaware Indians, gave a simple explanation for the string of disasters. The highway was built on a sacred Native American burial ground.

Mount Misery Road and Sweet Hollow Road

Hilly and full of unexpected twists and turns, Mount Misery Road got its name in horse-and-carriage times because it was such a treacherous road. It winds through **Huntington, New York**, the two meandering passages are so close together that they share some of the same ghost stories. Along Mount Misery Road and Sweet Hollow Road, drivers claim to have seen a phantom lady dressed in a hospital gown. Rumor has it she died when the asylum she was in burned down. Since then, she's been haunting the roads at night. She often appears at the edge of the forest, but when passengers turn to catch a second look, she's gone. Sometimes, she leaps out in front of cars, which leads to sudden, jolting stops and freaky accidents.

Also lurking in the woods of Mount Misery is the Hell Hound, a beast with red eyes and black fur. We've been told that anyone who sees the creature is doomed to die soon after.

There's even talk of a ghost policeman who is eternally on duty in these haunted hills. Fortunately, it's easy to recognize the undead patrolman. The back of his head is missing!

Route 666

If someone named a road "Flying Ghost Zebra Street," do you think police would start getting reports about a winged, striped, horse-shaped phantom? We're not sure, but we think that it would be an interesting experiment. And it wouldn't be the first time that a road's name led to legends. The highway planners who named **Arizona's** Route 666 didn't have the "Mark of the Beast" from the Book of Revelations in mind. They picked the name because the highway was the sixth branch of Route 66. They should have given the matter a little more thought. . . . Since its name conjured images of satanic rituals, local townspeople began calling the stretch of road "The Devil's Highway." Before long, Route 666 was widely believed to be cursed. Frightened motorists spotted all sorts of hellish creations—flaming ghost trucks and demon dogs with yellow eyes. There are tales about an apparition of a young girl who wanders along the highway in the dead of night. When drivers stop to help her, she vanishes. And there are legends about spirits who appear in front of speeding cars, hoping to cause crashes.

The curse of Route 666 became so well known that the name of the section of highway was finally changed. Maps of Arizona now refer to the road as Highway 191 and the part that runs through **Utah** is called New 491/Old 666. However, the name change hasn't put an end to the car wrecks and weird sightings. The curse remains.

Bloody Bucket Road

You won't find Bloody Bucket Road on any street signs in **Wauchula, Florida**, but ask around and everyone will know where the road is. They'll also tell you some horrifying tales about how Bloody Bucket Road got its sinister nickname. One story goes that a midwife went insane because she couldn't have children of her own. Mad with jealousy, she began killing babies immediately after they were born. One day, she discovered that her cleaning bucket was filled with blood. She grabbed it, ran to a bridge, and dumped the blood in the water below. But when she got back home, as soon as she set the bucket down it began to fill up again. The midwife knew what was happening. The bucket was filling with the blood of the babies she had murdered! Frantically, the midwife tried to get rid of the evidence, but no matter how many bucketfuls of blood she emptied into the river, when she returned home the bucket would fill again. This went on for days. Finally, on one trip, she slipped and fell into the river, never to be heard from again. The water ran red with blood for days.

Haunted Highways

Here are some haunted roads along with eyewitness accounts from a few of our Weird correspondents:

In the deep forests of **Carter County, Tennessee** lies the infamous Dark Hollow Road. As you drive along it past Dark Hollow Cemetery, it is said you'll feel a mysterious bump as if somebody had jumped into your backseat. It's the restless spirit of a woman named Delinda, who was buried in the cemetery more than a hundred years ago.

"My husband thought the legend was just a big story, so we drove slowly down the road. Suddenly the car began bucking and jumping. This continued until we reached the end of the area. I was shaken and asked my husband not to return home through Dark Hollow. He said he wasn't driving an extra ten miles and turned the car around. The car began jumping and lurching again as soon as we reached the haunted area."

If you travel down Stone Church Road, which is about ten miles from **Bartonville, Illinois**, you may run into the ghost of a man who's stuck by the side of the road with his car.

"One night my friends and I got the guts to check it out. We saw a car parked on the side and a man in the street. He wouldn't move. My friend got out and asked the guy what his problem was. The guy just looked at him without saying a word. Then suddenly, the guy was gone."

Meanwhile, in **Newtown, Pennsylvania**, there's Hansell Road. If you park along the side of the road at night, you may see a green mist followed by a black, shadowy entity, which is said to be the spirits of some kids who were murdered by an evil landowner for trespassing.

"We parked the car on the grass shoulder and sat on the hood for about twenty minutes. Then a red, glowing orb began coming out of the woods from the left side of the road. It bobbed slightly up and down about fifty feet ahead of us. It became two red, glowing orbs floating about six feet from the ground. They bobbed until they stopped in front of us and they stayed there. Then they disappeared."

People in **Jacksonville, North Carolina**, say that Highway 24 is haunted. The road is said to have been a Civil War trail used by the Union army, where they slaughtered a whole company of Confederate soldiers.

"My car's headlights dimmed real low; then the radio faded to nothing. At first I thought my car was breaking down, but then the gas pedal hit the floor by itself and the car took off straight for a tree. Right before I hit the tree, the car came to a dead stop and over the radio I heard a faint voice say, "Curse the living who mock this road.""

Green Hand Bridge

Crossing over Cane Creek in **Lancaster, South Carolina**, is a one-lane trestle called Green Hand Bridge. The name may sound funny at first, but if you saw a ghostly green hand rising up from the depths of the creek, you might not be so quick to laugh. Years ago, a few local men were hanging out on the bridge when they spotted it. Terrified, they spread the story around and the legend of Green Hand Bridge was born.

According to town folklore, this hand belongs to a British soldier who fought during the American Revolution. During a small skirmish in Lancaster, his arm was sliced off by a sharp saber. We're not sure if the armless soldier survived, but we've been told that his severed arm fell into the water below Green Hand Bridge. Apparently the arm doesn't realize that the war ended more than 200 years ago. Townspeople insist that the arm is still fighting. They say that sometimes it pops up swinging a sword. Other times it emerges from the water empty-handed.

The arm doesn't realize the war ended more than 200 years ago. It continues to fight ... sometimes with sword in hand!

Mitchell Bridge

It is said that a headless horseman haunts Mitchell Bridge near **Chatsworth, Georgia**. If you see this ghost on a misty night, you may be tempted to run away. But try and stick around, because a run-in with this particular headless spirit might be very rewarding. Here's the story: The phantom used to be a rich miser who hoarded his money and buried it in a secret place. He won't be able to rest in peace until someone finds it. And so, he haunts Mitchell Bridge chasing passersby, hoping to lead them to his buried treasure.

The only problem is that so many people have heard the tale that, if the headless horseman actually showed up, he'd probably have half of the town of Chatsworth chasing after him!

If you have the courage to wait ... you may hear the screams....

The Screaming Bridge

Like many haunted spots, the Screaming Bridge in **Arlington, Texas**, is extremely difficult to find. We asked around and everyone gave us conflicting directions. They also told us different stories, all involving a car accident that occurred in 1961.

A group of teenage girls were coming back from a high school football game (or perhaps they were returning after catching a flick at the local drive-in). They were excited. The night was dark. The bridge was narrow, and it all happened so fast that they never saw the other car coming. . . .

The road is closed off now, but we've heard that you can walk to the bridge through a path in River Legacy Park, although accounts vary. If you have the courage to wait there until midnight, you may hear the screams of the doomed teenagers. And if you peer into the water below, you may see glowing tombstones, one for each victim. You may even spot phantom headlights on the desolate road, because once a year, on the anniversary of the accident, the ghosts of the deceased replay the entire tragic scene.

Crybaby Bridges

If you're looking for a special setting for a strange and eerie tale, you can't do much better than a bridge in the middle of a forest. When you were little, you probably heard fairy tales about trolls living under bridges. You might have heard an old folk legend about witches being unable to cross a bridge. And maybe, just maybe, you heard about a bridge not far from where you live called the Crybaby Bridge.

There are crybaby bridges all over the United States. Some of them are quaint old covered bridges that look like sheds built across a river, where people on horseback used to shelter from the rain. Some of them are newer steel bridges, while others are made of stone. But no matter what they are made of, the legend goes that if you cross them late at night, you should stop and listen. When you do, you will hear faint cries—just like a baby crying for comfort.

Nobody knows where these sounds are coming from. Some people think that it may be a strange echo of the sound of the river, bouncing off the underside of the bridge. To others, the sound seems to be coming from the reeds nearby—and it's probably just toads. But there are some who think that these cries are the ghostly sound of an actual baby who died at the bridge. These are the people who keep the crybaby bridge legends alive.

We have heard many legends of crybaby bridges, with several examples in Ohio, Pennsylvania, Maryland, and New Jersey—and many other stories scattered throughout Weird America.

The Three Bridges of Eunice, Louisiana

In **Eunice, Louisiana,** there are three bridges on a stretch of road, and if you want to hear the sound of babies who are supposed to have died there, you must perform a strange ritual. You drive over the first bridge, turn around, honk the car horn, and drive back. When you come to the second bridge, you do the same thing—but twice over. That means two turn-arounds and two honks on the horn. At the third bridge—you guessed it—turn the car around three times and honk three times. It seems like a lot of effort, but sometimes, the weirdness is worth working for.

The Babies of Whipporwill Valley and Cooper Road

People in **Middletown, New Jersey** say strange things about Whipporwill Valley Road. They say that if you travel along the road at night as it dips down into the valley, you can hear a baby crying somewhere in the distance. And if you hear the baby's crying, your car will not be able to start up again. Not far away, on Cooper Road, there's a bridge that some claim is the source of the noise. If you go to the bridge at 1 AM, you can experience exactly the same thing.

Van Sant Bridge

We have heard two stories about the Van Sant Bridge in Solebury Township, near **New Hope, Pennsylvania**. One tells of a mother who was attacked by a stranger at the bridge. She and her baby were left for dead by the attacker, who was caught some time later and sentenced to die at the bridge. Another legend tells of a woman with twin babies who was abandoned and who took her children to the bridge, where all three of them died of despair. Obviously, both of these stories cannot be the true explanation of the weeping sounds at the Van Sant Bridge. Maybe neither of them is true. But those are the stories people tell.

Bridge over troubled water?

ANCIENT MYSTERIES

In our travels across America, we've come across many traces of ancient civilizations, and we often find ourselves at a loss for words. Sure, we all know that Columbus discovered the New World in 1492, but then what's up with the ancient Roman coin a woman in Georgia found while gardening? How did it get there? Could this coin be proof that the Romans came to America long before Columbus did? This is just one example of how, when it comes to ancient America, there are way more questions than answers—and the answers, when there are any, seem to contradict what we've learned in history class.

Mysterious Mounds

When American settlers were heading west, they stumbled upon awesome man-made mounds of earth. Then, they racked their brains trying to figure out what culture could possibly have created them. They quickly dismissed Native Americans as being too primitive and instead concocted ridiculous theories to explain the mounds. Were they built by ancient Egyptians, who had somehow found a way to American soil? Or maybe they were proof of some mythical advanced society that had sunk into the ocean? (The Lost City of Atlantis!)

In 1894, two men came along to set the record straight. In a study for the Bureau of American Ethnology, Cyrus Thomas and William H. Holmes confirmed that artifacts from mounds in **Illinois** were associated with Native American rituals. Thomas and Holmes also reported that certain tribes in southeastern parts of the United States were still building mounds. Still, many mysteries about the structures remain unsolved. How were they made? Why were they made? And is it possible that there are more ancient mounds hidden underneath our towns and cities?

Dickson Mounds

In the mid 1800s, William Dickson bought some land in Fulton County, near **Lewistown, Illinois**. Planning to build an orchard, he started clearing the land and uprooting trees. That's when he began to find human skeletons.

He had accidentally found a Native American burial mound. Instead of burying the dead in plots with stone markers, many tribes arranged corpses within a circle of land and then buried the entire mound. William Dickson's son, Don, became fascinated by the burial mound. A chiropractor by trade, Don Dickson began excavating the mound in his spare time. Soon after, he covered the mound with a tent and began charging visitors admission. Don Dickson ran the Dickson Mounds Museum until he sold the land to the state of Illinois in 1945. The bones remained on view for decades to come. But in recent times, Native Americans began protesting the exhibit. They thought that it was disrespectful that an ancient burial site was open to the public. Finally, in 1992, the government of Illinois placed a concrete slab over the dead, so they are now buried for good. Even though the tombs are closed, the museum continues to operate and has fascinating exhibits on twelve thousand years of Native American history in the Illinois River Valley.

Cahokia Mounds

The Great Pyramid of Giza in Egypt is considered one of the Seven Wonders of the Ancient World. Now, we would never knock the Great Pyramid, but we think that the ancient world left us with lots and lots of wonders. So why stop at seven?

Near **Collinsville, Illinois**, is one of the most magnificent mound complexes in the United States. It's the remains of a large, bustling Native American city called Cahokia. Scientists speculate that tens of thousands of Cahokians once lived there, and the city once consisted of more than 120 mounds. At the center is Monk's Mound. It spans sixteen acres, which makes it even bigger at its base than the Great Pyramid of Giza. And it has a built-in staircase for easy access. At the top, archeologists have uncovered pipes for tobacco rituals, as well as pottery, and birds and snakes made of copper. These discoveries imply that a sacred temple once sat on the mound.

There are many unanswered questions about Cahokia. Why are there no records and no legends from other local tribes describing the enormous ancient city? And what happened to the Cahokians? All we know for sure is that the Cahokians were an impressive bunch. And we would definitely include the Cahokia Mounds on our list of Weird Wonders of the Ancient World.

Check it out! www.cahokiamounds.org

Serpent Mound

Besides building mounds for burial, mound builders constructed gigantic tributes to the creatures they worshipped. These strangely shaped structures are known as effigy mounds. One of the most spectacular examples is the Serpent Mound in **Adams County, Ohio**. The Serpent Mound lies in a fifty-four-acre park and was most likely built by the Adena Indians, who are known to have been expert mound builders. The entire effigy mound was created inside a crater, which was formed by a meteorite thousands of years ago.

From head to tail, the snake is about a quarter of a mile long, or 1,330 feet. It begins (or ends) with a spiraling tail. The body curves back and forth, winding gracefully through the grassy valley, and ends (or begins) with a huge mouth, wide open and about to swallow something that looks like a giant egg. Or perhaps it's supposed to be the body of a frog. Or the sun . . . In any case, the snake looks very hungry.

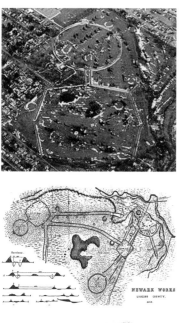

Octagons, Circles & Underwater Panthers

In **Newark, Ohio**, there's another effigy mound known as the Alligator Mound. And if it doesn't look like an alligator to you, you're not alone. Some experts believe that it represents a fierce beast from Native American mythology called the Underwater Panther. Close by is a huge, perfectly circular wall of earth, which is connected to an even bigger embankment, shaped like an octagon. We have no clue what these walls are for, but it's possible that the entire complex is some sort of ancient lunar observatory.

Researchers believe that the mysterious objects were made by the Hopewell, a lost civilization that was responsible for many geometric earthworks around Ohio. No one knows why the Hopewell vanished more than 1,600 years ago. In fact, no one knows much at all about the Hopewell.

N'omi Greber, an archeologist at the Cleveland Museum of Natural History, spoke to Cleveland's *The Plain Dealer* about the ancient culture. "We know more about the Egyptians and the Assyrians than the people who were in our own backyard," explained Greber. "They left no writing that we know of. They just left octagons, rectangles, and circles. You try to figure out what it means and it drives you up a tree after a while. Why did they do it? Why, why, why? Nobody knows."

Petroglyphs and Pictographs

Ancient Native Americans were not only expert mound builders, they were also accomplished artists. And their medium of choice was stone. They painted on rock surfaces to produce pictographs, and they carved symbols to create elaborate objects called *petroglyphs*.

The symbols and paintings are now impossible to interpret, but that only makes them more intriguing. For all we know, these pictographs and petroglyphs might be ancient graffiti, saying nothing more than, "I WUZ HERE," or they might offer some mystical insight that's infinitely more valuable.

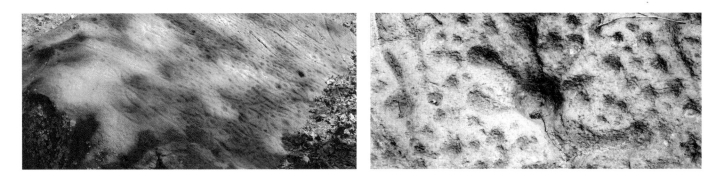

Judaculla Rock

One of the most mysterious petroglyphs in the country, Judaculla Rock, can be found in the mountains of Jackson County, near **Cullowhee, North Carolina**. The carvings on Judaculla Rock are a mixed bag of lines and circles, doodles that look like stick figures, and others that just look like doodles.

The soapstone boulder where these petroglyphs appear got its name from an old Cherokee legend about a "slant-eyed" giant called Tsul'kalu'. According to the story, the giant's mother was a comet and his father was thunder, and he had seven fingers on each hand. One day, he scratched the boulder with his fingers or toes, and he accidentally created the mysterious markings.

We love stories about seven-fingered giants, but we were hoping for a more plausible theory to explain the carvings. What are these lines and circles supposed to represent? Is it some kind of a map? Perhaps it's a form of prehistoric Cherokee writing, which tells an old tribal story. A paranormal group based in Asheville, North Carolina, suggested another possibility. It's convinced that the etchings on the stone are pictures of microscopic organisms—amoebas, bacteria, and hydras with outstretched tentacles. Skeptics, of course, quickly dismissed this theory. The rock was carved thousands of years before microscopes were invented. How could the carvers know what microorganisms looked like? The paranormal group had an easy answer: the markings were made by ancient astronauts. In other words, thousands of years ago, space aliens came to North Carolina and covered a boulder with squiggly etchings of microorganisms.

Check it out! www.judacullarock.com

Cave of the White Shaman

The young brave said to the old shaman, "In my vision, I died and rose above my body in flight. Soon I was passing over the village, and I could see my friends going on their day. Suddenly I realized that I had been transformed into a crow, and that is why I could fly.
Was I really flying?"

"Yes," answered the old shaman.

"Could my friends see me flying?"

The old shaman looked at him sternly and said, "What difference does that make? It is the individual experience, not what we want others to see or think that is important."

This tale comes from Jim Zintgraff of the Rock Art Foundation, and it was inspired by the pictographs inside the Cave of the White Shaman in Texas. These aboriginal cave paintings by the Pecos people describe the spiritual journeys of their shaman. In the photo (on the right), the shaman is the elongated figure, flying upward. He has claws for hands and feet, and he has no head. The black smudgy thing beside him is his body, which he's leaving behind. All sorts of wonders are on view inside the caves in the Lower Pecos region of **southwest Texas**.

Track Rock Gap

In the Chattahoochee National Forest, near the town of **Blairsville, Georgia**, are six soapstone boulders with hundreds of symbols carved into them. Unlike most petroglyphs, it's obvious what these ones represent. They are perfect imitations of animal tracks.

Horse, buffalo, deer, and rabbit footprints are all faithfully rendered. And human footprints are depicted as well, in twenty-six different sizes. One measures seventeen inches and is thought to be the print of a giant.

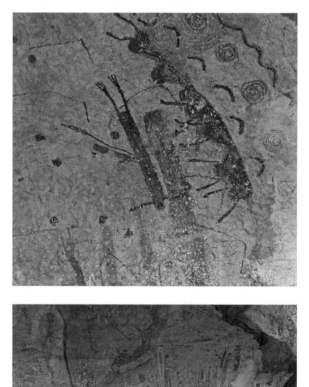

The Mysterious Land of Gungywamp

Gungywamp is a weird archaeological site on top of a cliff in **Groton, Connecticut**. Scattered about Gungywamp are all sorts of ancient ruins—prehistoric rock piles, stone chambers, mounds of earth, and petroglyph-bearing slabs. There's also a circle of stones laid out inside a larger circle of stones. Was it once used as some kind of religious altar or was it created for some other reason? (A campfire circle? A bull's-eye for an ancient game of rock toss?)

No one can agree on who made these structures or what they were used for. Still, the weirdest Gungywamp tales are about a mysterious power that pervades the area, especially at the spot called the Cliff of Tears. Visitors who have stood on this rock ledge claim to have felt strangely sad. If you're brave enough to face the Cliff of Tears, you can take a guided tour through Gungywamp.

Check it out!
www.gungywamp.com

America's Stonehenge

A megalithic structure is a man-made formation of large rocks. Stonehenge, on Salisbury Plain in Southern England, is the most famous example in the world. But we have plenty of megalithic creations in the United States. In fact, one is known as America's Stonehenge, and it's a must-see for anyone with a good appreciation for ancient enigmas.

America's Stonehenge is a long-abandoned rock village that sits on a granite hilltop in **Salem, New Hampshire**. Discovered by farmer Jonathon Pattee in 1826, it's generally thought to be more than 4,000 years old. With rooms known as the Oracle Chamber and the Watch House, this meandering stone fort gives off a spooky vibe. So it's not surprising that it was featured in the famous weird tale "The Dunwich Horror" by H. P. Lovecraft. If you visit America's Stonehenge, you might be surprised to find a fenced animal enclosure. And if you peek inside, you'll see . . . alpacas! We're not sure how these llama look-alikes are related to prehistoric ruins, but you might want to stop for a while to admire the adorable fuzzy beasts. But don't stay too long—the best is yet to come!

The man-made rock formation is massive and impressive—a mazelike network of stone chambers and underground tunnels. Some of the stones are gigantic, weighing up to eleven tons. It's hard to imagine who could have constructed this megalithic wonder.

Most scientists believe that the site was built by prehistoric Native Americans, probably the ancestors of the Pennacooks. However, many people disagree and have put forth a long list of alternate possibilities, such as Irish Culdee monks, Celts, and Phoenicians. There's also confusion about why the structure was built. Experts agree that the site had been carefully laid out so that it could be used as an observatory for solar and lunar events. But did it have other uses? Did people once live there? Or had it been designed for some kind of ancient religious ceremonies?

A granite table on the ground seems like it could have been a sacrificial stone. A gutter had been carved around the edge. Was this groove made so that sacrificial blood would drain off properly? Or was the table an ancient cutting board used in food preparation?

The longer you stay, the more questions you'll have. To our knowledge, there are only two things certain about America's Stonehenge: the alpacas are cute, and its former name was more appropriate. It used to be called Mystery Hill.

Check it out! www.stonehengeusa.com

Tripod Rock

Tripod Rock in **Morris County, New Jersey**, is a fascinating geological phenomenon that raises the intriguing question, "How'd that really big rock get balanced on top of those little tiny rocks?"

Many scientists believe that the big rock was carried by a glacier and was deposited on the little rocks when the glacier melted. But the weird thing is that there are two smaller Tripod Rocks about ten feet away from this big Tripod Rock. That seems like a tricky stunt for a glacier to pull off. Perhaps there's another explanation. Is this a signpost created by some very strong ancient Native Americans? A rock pile made by a giant baby?

Here's another impressive example of "How'd that really big rock get there?" Called Balanced Rock, it can be found in **North Salem, New York**.

Check it out!
www.tripodrock.org

Blue Mounds Mystery Stones

One of the simplest and most elegant weird rock formations in the country can be found in Blue Mounds State Park in **Luverne, Minnesota**—a perfect line of stones, stretching from east to west, 1,250 feet long.

We don't know who put them there. And we don't know when, although some have speculated that the Blue Mounds rocks have been around for a very long time. We also don't know why these stones were carefully lined up in a row. The only clue we have is that, every year, on the first day of spring and fall, the line points directly to the sunrise in the morning and to the sunset at night. Perplexing and quietly mysterious, this long line of rocks has earned the nickname Minnesota's Stonehenge.

Who Came Before Columbus?

Christopher Columbus has had it tough lately. Not long ago, the Italian adventurer was revered as a great explorer, who discovered the "New World" and proved that the earth wasn't flat. Not anymore . . .

By the time Columbus set sail from Spain, the flat-earth theory had been abandoned, and educated people knew that the world was round. In fact, more than 500 years beforehand, a Greek astronomer named Eratosthenes had predicted the earth's circumference with surprising accuracy.

And how do you discover a place that's already inhabited anyway? Yet, even discounting Native American populations, it seems that Columbus came to North America relatively late in the game. Travelers from all over the world may have passed by long before him. Since they predated Columbus, these mysterious ancient visitors are often labeled "pre-Columbian." Excavations by archeologists have unearthed artifacts from many different non-Native American, pre-Columbian cultures. Other discoveries have been made by normal people digging around in their backyards. Prehistoric coins. Mysterious tablets with strange inscriptions. These objects have made it very difficult for us to answer a very simple question: "Who came here and when?"

Visitors from China?

Did Chinese adventurer and Buddhist missionary Hui-Shen visit America in 458 CE? If he did, he beat Columbus by more than a thousand years! His exploits are described in the travel account *Chu I Chuan: The History of the Liang Dynasty*. According to the book, Hui-Shen spent forty years living in a place that he called Fu-Sang. After returning to China, he described the strange customs of the inhabitants. Was this mysterious place the coast of California? Ancient Chinese coins and cave drawings found in **California** and **Nevada** could back up this theory. Plus, a map found in a Korean antique store in 1972 refers to Fu-Sang. This map is known as the "Harris Map" because it was found by a man named Hendon Mason Harris, who later went on to write a book called *The Asiatic Fathers of America*.

The map places Fu-Sang near an area called Double Rainbow Land. And Mr. Harris was convinced that he knew the whereabouts of this magical place. "We could suppose that it was northeast of Southern California and toward the Grand Canyon," he said. "Rainbows in the desert are very lovely and often appear in double form."

Visitors from Scandinavia?

Olof Ohman, a Swedish immigrant, was digging on his farm in **Kensington, Minnesota**, in 1898, when he unearthed a slab of graywacke stone covered with inscriptions. The runes, or ancient letters, were written in an old Scandinavian language.

Here's the translation:
Eight Goths and twenty-two Norwegians on an exploration journey from Vinland to the west. We had camp by 2 skerries one day's journey north from this stone. We were to fish one day after we came home found 10 men red with blood and dead AVM (Ave Maria)

On the side of the stone: Have 10 men by the sea to look after our ships 14 days' travel from this island Year 1362.

1362! That would mean this runestone is rock-solid evidence that Scandinavian travelers wandered through Minnesota 130 years before Columbus landed in the Bahamas. But not so fast! The Kensington Runestone may have been a hoax perpetrated by its finder. Did the farmer create a fake runestone to boost Scandinavian pride in Minnesota? Was he hoping to use the ploy to make money? Experts have been arguing over the Kensington Runestone for more than a hundred years. Those who believe that it's authentic have tried to unravel its mysteries. "Vinland" was the name the Vikings used for North America. For one of the translators of the stone, Hjalmar Holand, "Red with Blood" implied murder. For author Thomas Reiergord, who wrote about the runestone in 2001, it meant disease. He believes that the bubonic plague was responsible for the ten deaths described on the rock.

Was the Kensington Runestone left behind by ancient explorers? If so, what was its purpose? A prehistoric diary entry? A warning? Or was the runestone a clever fake?

The only certainty is that people will be guessing for years to come. You can visit the Kensington Runestone at the Runestone Museum in **Alexandria, Minnesota** and guess along.

Check it out!
www.runestonemuseum.org

Heavener Runestone

This slab of runestone found in **Heavener, Oklahoma**, was first discovered by the Choctaw tribe inside a ravine atop Poteau Mountain. They had never seen the writing before. When white settlers made their way to the area in the 1870s, they were equally baffled. The Smithsonian Institution determined that the symbols were ancient Norse runes. But what do the runes stand for? Some researchers thought they represented a date: November 11, 1012; however, later experts claim they stand for "Glome Valley." This could mean that not only did Vikings explore as far as Oklahoma, but they settled there! These days, the rock is the centerpiece of the Heavener Runestone State Park.

The Mystery Stone, located at the base of Hidden Mountain in New Mexico, contains carved letters that look like they come from an ancient Phoenician or Hebrew alphabet. Who wrote these letters? Was it an ancient Greek explorer? A member of the Ten Lost Tribes of Israel? Or is it a hoax? Nobody knows.

Visitors from Greece and Rome?

We've heard stories from all around the country about ancient Greek and Roman artifacts turning up in unexpected places. In **Texas**, Roman coins were found buried inside a Native American mound, and the remains of a sunken ship—possibly Roman—were pulled out of Galveston Bay. In **Olney, Illinois**, Russell Burrows discovered a cave by accidentally falling into it. Fortunately, his clumsiness paid off. In the rubble, he found ancient objects from Rome, Greece, and Egypt. Many archaeologists have dismissed Burrow's Cave as a hoax. Others are convinced that these findings are real and prove that we had visitors long before Columbus sailed to our shores.

Finally, in **Columbus**, Georgia, a Roman coin, almost 2,000 years old, was found in a woman's garden, and another, even older, was found in a construction site. These discoveries raise a perplexing question: why have so many pre-Columbian relics turned up in Columbus, Georgia, a town named after the explorer? An odd coincidence, don't you think?

TOMBSTONE TOURS

Cemeteries are sad and often creepy places. But did you know that they can also make you laugh and ask, "What's that all about?" They really can, and the reason is simple: some cool people have fun with the statues or gravestones they leave behind, and they try to make them fun for everyone else. That's why so many people enjoy visiting cemeteries. So, join us as we jump into the Weirdmobile for a trip to some of the strange sights in our nation's cemeteries. Prepare for a smile or two and a good scare along the way!

Tombstone's Tombstones

In the late 1800s, Tombstone was a Wild West boomtown where gunfights and outlaws filled its Boothill Graveyard with more than 300 dead in less than six years. The victims of the famous Gunfight at the O.K. Corral lie here under a stone that reads: Murdered on the Streets of Tombstone.

The most famous epitaphs, however, are a bit funnier. In 1882, George Johnson was accused of stealing a horse—a crime that carried the death penalty. He insisted he had bought the horse from the real thief, and he was telling the truth, but in Tombstone they didn't wait long before hanging the condemned. They discovered George was innocent after his execution, and so you can see this epitaph in Boothill Graveyard:

Here lies
George Johnson
Hanged by mistake
1882
—

He was right
We was wrong
But we strung him up
And now he's gone

Another tombstone is that of Lester Moore. He was a Wells Fargo agent—which was like being a UPS or FedEx deliveryman in the old days—who was shot by a man who was angry when he found his package was damaged.

Here lies
Lester Moore
Four slugs from a .44
No Les
No more

Check it out!

www.boothillgraves.com

Crazy Inscriptions

The words inscribed on tombstones are called *epitaphs*, and like all writing assignments, they have certain rules. Epitaphs need to include the name or names of the people buried there. They should include dates of birth and death. After that, there's room to be creative.

Daniel Steven Burley's grave, Forest Lawn Cemetery, **Glendale, California**

John "Jack" Wagner's grave, St. Joseph's Cemetery, **Toms River, New Jersey**

Vince E. Bushey's grave, Forest Lawn Cemetery, **Glendale, California**

Why live and be miserable when you can be buried comfortably for a few bucks plus Erie County sales tax?
—Lee Neal Jr.'s grave, St John's Lutheran Cemetery, **Cheektowaga, New York**

Here lies old Caleb Ham
By trade a bum.
When he died the devil cried
Come, Caleb, come
—Caleb Ham's grave,
Hollis, New Hampshire

Office Upstairs
—Dr. Fred Roberts's grave, Maple Grove Cemetery, **Hoosick Falls, New York**

Here lies as silent clay
Miss Arabella Young
Who on the 21st of May 1771
Began to hold her tongue
—Arabella Young's grave, **Hatfield, Massachusetts**

Near by these gray rocks
Enclosed in a box
Lies hatter Cox who died
of small pox
—Mr. Cox's grave, **Rainsford Island, Massachusetts**

This is on me.
—On a boulder marking William Rothwell's grave, **Pawtucket, Rhode Island**

I was somebody
Who, is no business of yours.
—Somebody's grave,
Stowe, Vermont

What's My Line?

Back in your grandparents' day, there was a TV quiz show called *What's My Line?* In this show, the quizmaster introduced a stranger and with a few clues and questions, the audience had to guess what job he or she did. Wandering around cemeteries can feel a bit like that. Of course, some grave markers make it pretty easy for you to figure out a person's profession!

Hey! Ho! . . . Let's Go!

Hollywood Forever Cemetery in **Los Angeles, California** is full of movie stars from the 1920s right through to the present day. But not everyone there is a movie star. Two members of the classic punk band the Ramones are also there. Guitarist Johnny Ramone had a big bronze statue of himself made. It stands on a block of granite, clutching a low-slung guitar in a classic rock-star pose. It's easy to imagine what song he's playing—it could be "Blitzkrieg Bop," "Rockaway Beach," or any of the other fast and fun songs the band made famous. The grave of the band's bass player, Dee Dee Ramone, shows what looks like the presidential seal—but it's actually the band's logo. Underneath is the joke epitaph, "Ok ... I gotta go now."

Herman the Diver

His mustache and beard make him look a bit like Colonel Sanders from KFC, but Herman Wolter from Philadelphia didn't fry chickens for a living. Just take a look at his bulky suit, the air tubes, the straps, the rope, and the heavy lead weights around his waist. If that doesn't give you a clue, take a look at the helmet resting by his foot. Herman was a deep-sea diver and when he died in 1901, he chose to be remembered that way. His statue looks out almost longingly onto the main road that runs past the Fernwood Cemetery. It's a long hike from **Philadelphia** to the ocean, and he has a lot of heavy gear to carry.

Check it out! www.hollywoodforever.com

Shocking!

You can see what Sal Giardino did for a living before you can even read his name on the base of his black marble grave marker. It's in Laurel Grove Cemetery in **Totowa, New Jersey,** and it's shaped like a lightbulb. It shows a picture of a fist clutching sparks of lightning. There is a two-socket power outlet carved into the base. And if that isn't enough of a hint, there's a caption in gold letters declaring: World's Greatest Electrician.

The Granite Grand

It's easy to figure out what Madge Ward did for a living. Just go to Rose Hill Cemetery in **Tyler, Texas**, and look for the largest monument you can find. It's an eight-foot-tall piano that weighs twenty-five tons, and Madge Ward was laid to rest inside it. The granite grand piano took more than a year to design and build. Madge saved her earnings as an entertainer and piano teacher to pay for it.

The Metal-Working Marvel

William Jennings Wedekind was a blacksmith in **Hagerstown, Indiana**, who won a gold medal for making horseshoes at the Chicago World's Fair in 1892. He returned to his small town to continue his life, but people kept coming to watch the man the newspapers were calling, "The World's Greatest Horseshoer." They also wanted to buy the display case that contained the tools he used to win his gold medal. He was offered anywhere from $20,000 to $100,000—that's a lot of money now, but it was worth a lot more in the early 1900s, when candy bars cost only five cents. He never did sell the display case. He hammered away at his anvil for another thirty years, and when he died, he was buried under a statue of it.

Elephant's Memory

In **Moultrie, Georgia**, there's an elephant on a gravestone, but don't let that fool you—it's not an elephant's grave. It's the grave of a circus owner named William Duggan, who was born in 1899. He ran away with the circus at the age of twelve, and his first job was taking care of elephants. He worked hard and eventually owned his own big top, the Hagen-Wallace Circus. Mr. Duggan's son thought that the best way for people to remember his father would be a statue of his father's favorite elephant, a baby called Nancy.

Tricky Business

There's only one place we know of where it's not terribly disrespectful to write the words, "Ricki Dunn was a thief!" on a gravestone. It's in the town of **Colon, Michigan**. Other mean-spirited words such as "pickpocket" and "fraud" are dotted around on stones throughout the Lakeside Cemetery. But it's all okay, because this is the final resting place of more than twenty stage magicians, and if there's one thing you need to succeed in that career (aside from conjuring skills), it's a great sense of humor.

Tales from the Crypt

Has anyone ever told you a story that made your heart beat faster with fear? Us, too! And many of the best of them took place in graveyards. These stories often center around a distinctive statue or monument and the strange story behind it.

Black Aggie, the Living Statue

What could be scarier than a graveyard statue that comes to life at night? We can think of only one thing: a graveyard statue that comes to life at night to hunt down and kill whomever stands in its way. And that's the legend of Black Aggie, the killer statue. The original Black Aggie statue, her eyes covered by a veil, sat for a century in Druid Ridge Cemetery, north of **Baltimore, Maryland**. For those hundred years, people swapped scary stories about her, visited her at night, and dared each other to peek under her veil or sit on her lap. Visitors would also wonder who this woman was and how she had met her end.

Some people said she was a sad woman who died of a broken heart because her husband was cruel. Other people said she was a single woman who was killed by a mob. But everyone agreed on one thing: because she died young, she was angry at the living and wanted them to join her in death.

But suddenly, one day in the 1980s, the statue disappeared. All that remained was a scar on the marble platform where she had sat, and the name "Agnus" carved on it. That was when everyone started saying the statue had stood up and was wandering around the graveyard, stalking her next victim.

The real truth behind the statue is not as scary as the stories. The statue was donated to the Smithsonian Institute in Washington D.C. She now sits in the courtyard of the Dolley Madison House near the White House. And to top it all off, the statue didn't even mark a woman's grave at all. A general from the Civil War named Felix Agnus bought the statue from a local sculptor and put it on his own grave, long before he actually died. He just liked the mysterious and spooky way it looked!

The Witch's Chair

You often see marble chairs in cemeteries. They usually mark the grave of a mother or father, and they remind visitors that in a house somewhere, there is an empty chair where the person who died used to sit. Gravesite chairs also appear in graveyard stories. One especially creepy tale tells of the witch's chair, which we've heard from two different graveyards—one in Michigan and the other in Pennsylvania.

In Brookside Cemetery in **Tecumseh, Michigan**, you can find an old-fashioned easy chair with the name "Stacy" on it. They call it the Witch's Chair, but there was never a witch called Stacy. Stacy was the last name of a large family headed up by the man in charge of the local post office—Alphonso Stacy. The story starts more than a hundred years ago, when Stacy's daughter, Loanna, worked with him in the post office. People began talking about her behind her back, saying she was a witch. Residents began blaming her whenever anybody got sick or when their farm animals died. Loanna never married, and as her family died off, she was left to live alone in the huge mansion on the town's main street. Years later, people say her ghost still walks through the old Stacy mansion at night. And in the graveyard near where she was buried, her empty-chair grave marker is not always empty.

Six hundred miles away in **Bristol, Pennsylvania**, there's another witch's chair. This one is made out of iron and stands right in front of the grave of Merritt P. Wright in St. James Episcopal Cemetery. Local legend has it that if you sit in this chair at midnight on any night during October, a witch's arms will come out and grab you. The local newspaper once reported that someone who lives near the graveyard saw a woman sitting in the chair at night and assumed that she was testing out the legend. He was about to make a call, but the woman vanished before his eyes. Was this the ghost of Mrs. Wright? Was it the mysterious witch? We don't know. But we don't think we'll be visiting that graveyard any night in October—just to be safe.

Crystal Shrine Grotto

By now, you will have noticed that there's more to cemeteries than headstones and angel statues. But even we were surprised by what was in store at **Memphis, Tennessee's** Memorial Park Cemetery. For one thing, it has a fake oak tree in it with realistic broken branches and insect holes. But it has a plaque on it saying it's made of metal and concrete. It's called Abraham's Oak, and it's the work of a sculptor named Dionicio Rodriguez, who built the tree and a nearby grotto in the 1930s. The grotto is even more amazing than the tree. Its concrete walls are encrusted with crystals, which is why they call it the Crystal Shrine Grotto. It's nice and cool down there even on the hottest summer days, and it's full of sculptures that show stories of Jesus from the New Testament. It's like an underground art gallery—so it's hard to imagine why anyone would build it in a cemetery in Tennessee. One thing's for sure: it's a one-of-a-kind place.

Check it out!
www.memorialparkfuneralandcemetery.com

A mausoleum is a building in a graveyard that usually looks like something from ancient Rome, with impressive columns and heavy doors and stained-glass windows. However, this mini-mausoleum in the old Elmwood Cemetery in **Charlotte, North Carolina,** is a granite log cabin dedicated to Henry Severs.

Living in Hope Cemetery

The fantastic stone carvers of **Barre, Vermont**, really had some fun in the town's famous landmark, Hope Cemetery. They filled the place with sculptures and gravestone pictures that you'll never find anywhere else in the world. Don't believe us? Just look around.

How many soccer-ball gravestones have you seen? We've seen only one, and it's right there in Hope Cemetery. The same goes for the granite biplane (that's an airplane with two-story wings) that you can see mounted on a statue of clouds. And the armchair with the name "Bettini" written on it looks almost comfy enough to watch TV in—except for the fact that it's made of solid granite.

Are you wondering why this little New England town has so many great sculptures in it? Well, it's called the Granite Capital of the World—they quarry the stone and make sculptures to export right there in the neighborhood. And obviously, they like to keep the best stuff close to home!

Joey Laquerre's Stock Car
What better way to celebrate the victories of a stock-car racer than to put a half-size replica of his car on top of his grave? That's what the widow of the local racing hero Armand "Joey" Laquerre thought. The marble statue that marks his final parking place is full of detail. You can even see the protective cage over the side windows and Joey's race-car number, 61, etched on the driver's side door.

A Stylish Ride to the Other Side

When Vikings died, they were pushed out to sea on a burning ship. The Egyptian pharaohs were put in their tombs with chariots to carry them to the afterlife. And the ancient Greeks were buried with coins to rent a ferry across the River Styx to the Underworld. All across history, people have associated death with a journey. It's no different in the United States today. Take a look at some of the ways we mark our cemeteries with methods of transportation.

Buried in Their Cars

Some people aren't just buried under replicas of cars—they're actually buried inside their cars. Here are a few examples:

George Swanson was a World War II veteran who loved to drive his white 1984 Corvette around **Pittsburgh, Pennsylvania**. Its license plate read HI PAL, which was George's greeting for everyone he met. When he died in 1994, his widow asked Brush Creek Cemetery to bury him inside his beloved car. A crane lowered the convertible into a deep hole, with George's ashes in an urn on the driver's seat.

Four years later, a retired policewoman named Rose Martin was buried inside a 1962 Corvair. That happened in the Pocasset Hill Cemetery in **Tiverton, Rhode Island**. They took out the engine and seats and cut a big hole in the car so that Rose's coffin could fit inside.

Ray Tse's Mercedes

Parked behind a huge marble mausoleum in Linden Park Cemetery in **New Jersey** is a white Mercedes-Benz 240 Diesel. Its front license plate bears the name of its owner, Ray Tse, but he never drove the car. Nobody has. In fact, even though it has stood there for more than thirty years, this car has never been given a ticket or towed. That's because it's carved out of a single block of granite.

Raymond Tse lived in Hong Kong, but he often visited his older brother David in New Jersey. David owned many luxury cars and promised Raymond a Mercedes when he turned seventeen. Tragically, Raymond died in a car accident in Hong Kong when he was only fifteen. But David kept his promise, and commissioned a granite car for his memorial. The hand-carved sculpture took a year to complete, and it's a life-sized replica with carved door handles, wheel treads, and windshield wipers.

Time Expired

This unique grave marker belongs to Barbarar Sue Manire and can be found in Highland Cemetery in **Okemah, Oklahoma**. It became the subject of millions of forwarded e-mails in 2007. This e-mail message tells the story of the tombstone:

"This lady had a great sense of humor and always used to say that when she died she wanted a parking meter on her grave that says 'Expired.' So her nephew got her one on eBay! She said that her grave is right by the road so everyone can see it and many people have stopped to get a chuckle."

For a last word, we'll leave it to Mel Blanc, the man who gave voice to Bugs Bunny, Daffy Duck, and dozens of other cartoon characters. He read the epitaph—that is now set in stone at the Hollywood Forever Cemetery in **Los Angeles, California**—at the end of thousands of cartoons in his Porky Pig voice:

THAT'S ALL, FOLKS!

INDEX

ACKNOWLEDGMENTS

Matt's

Books aren't like homework assignments. They're like projects that a whole class works on. The class responsible for this book is one of the most fun I've ever worked with. Mark Moran and Mark Sceurman keep our eyes focused on what's weird and what's funny. Every chapter that Randy Fairbanks wrote made me think, "I wish I'd written that! And if I keep quiet, maybe people will think I did!" More thanks go out to Emily Seese for holding things together, Ryan Doan for illustrating these pages and generally making everyone laugh, and to the field correspondents who keep sending reports back to Weird Central. Big thanks go out to Julia, Genevieve, Chris, Stephan, Danny and Nicole, and all the fourth and fifth graders who pass by me in school corridors, for reminding me how to have fun while I get the work done. And thanks to the shadowy figure of Joe Rhatigan, a mysterious figure who lurks in dark doorways in Weird North Carolina and waylays stray sentences as they pass by. They leave his presence some time later as fully polished prose, and we at Weird Central don't quite know how this happens. Keep it weird out there!

Randy's

This book for weird kids would not have been possible without the help of a lot of weird adults. Thanks to the Marks behind Weird NJ—Mark Moran and Mark Sceurman—for helping me exercise my Weird Eye, and to our editor Joe Rhatigan, who beautifully shaped our bizarre beast of a book. (Not an easy job! Like giving Bigfoot a haircut!) And to my fantastic collaborator, Matt Lake, for constantly raising the bar and keeping me updated on strange holidays. (If it's March 20, Happy Festival of Extraterrestrial Abductions Day!) Also, to the many writers who contributed to the Weird US book series, which is slowly taking over my library. Big muffler-man-sized hugs go out to my family and friends, especially to my wife, Elizabeth Applegate, who mulled over these words, gave me great comments, got rid of extraneous commas, and put smiley faces next to the funny parts. Finally, my gratitude goes out to all the kids who wrote to Weird NJ and to the Weird Club. Thanks for sending us your weird!

ABOUT
THE AUTHORS

Matt

The Biography of Mark Sceurman, Mark Moran, Matt Lake, and Randy Fairbanks

Mark Sceurman and Mark Moran started the Weird U.S. series of books, all of which deal with all the weird things you can find across the nation. Randy Fairbanks and Matt Lake wrote a few books in this series by themselves, and have written this book together. The Marks, Randy, and Matt think of themselves as average guys. They are an average of 5 feet 11 inches tall, and they have an average of one daughter and a quarter of a son each. On average, they were born in the middle of the Atlantic Ocean on June 17 1/2. This makes each of them a quarter of a Gemini, or half a twin apiece. The midpoint between where they all live—the place they call their "average home base"—is the dead center of the reservoir in Round Valley State Park. Their favorite activities include bike riding and reading and playing half a guitar each.

Yes, the Marks, Randy, and Matt are individually weird.

Randy

PHOTO CREDITS

SHOW US YOUR WEIRD!

Do you know of a weird site found somewhere in the United States, or can you tell us about a strange experience you've had? If so, we'd like to hear about it! We believe that every town has at least one great tale to tell, and we're listening. It could be a cursed road, a haunted grocery store, an odd character, or a bizarre historic event. In most cases, these tales are told only in the towns in which they originated. But why keep them to yourself when you could share them with all of America? So come on and fill us in on all the weirdness that's lurking in your backyard!

You can e-mail us at: editor@weirdUS.com

Or write to us at:
Weird U.S., P.O. Box 1346,
Bloomfield, NJ 07003
www.weirdus.com

Hey, you can also join our club for kids:
www.weirdclub.com